REGINALD HILL

FELL OF DARK

HARPER

Harper
An imprint of HarperCollins*Publishers*
77–85 Fulham Palace Road,
Hammersmith, London W6 8JB

www.harpercollins.co.uk

This paperback re-issue 2010

2

First published in Great Britain by
HarperCollins*Publishers* in 1971

Copyright © Reginald Hill 1971

Reginald Hill asserts the moral right to
be identified as the author of this work

A catalogue record for this book is
available from the British Library

ISBN: 978-0-00-733479-7

Set in Meridien by Palimpsest Book Production Ltd,
Grangemouth, Stirlingshire

Mixed Sources
Product group from well-managed
forests and other controlled sources
www.fsc.org Cert no. SW-COC-001806
© 1996 Forest Stewardship Council

For my mother

I wake and feel the fell of dark, not day.
What hours, O what black hours we have spent
This night! What sights you, heart, saw.

- *G.M. Hopkins*

ONE

I possess the Englishman's usual ambivalent attitude to the police. They are at once protectors and persecutors. They tell you the way, but they make you feel guilty for asking.

I watch, or I used to watch, most of the 'realistic' TV series based on police-work with that fascinated revulsion which makes them so compelling. But I had often wondered why innocent people allowed themselves so readily to be manipulated by the police, why invitations to proceed to the station were not more frequently refused.

Now I knew. Or at least I knew in my case. From the moment we had been stopped, a terrible passivity had begun to settle on me. It was a feeling that the quickest and surest way of getting back to normal was to sit very quietly and do as I was requested. It was rather like a child with a visit to the dentist in the offing, sitting as small as possible, hoping to be unnoticed, trying desperately not to obtrude.

There hadn't been any suggestion that we were doing anything but 'helping with enquiries'. No question of our guilt or innocence seemed to be involved. I didn't see how it possibly could be involved. But I didn't feel innocent. And with Peter it was worse. Sitting pushed up against the car door (locked, I suspected), his unseeing gaze fixed on the rain-spattered window-pane, he didn't even look innocent. I was much more concerned about him than I was about myself.

At least that was what I liked to think. That was what I had been telling myself for a long time now. It was true! I assured myself fiercely. Of course it was true!

If I looked back into the past, I would be able to prove quite convincingly that what had brought me to this police car, boring steadily through the rain up into the Lakeland fells, was a combination of my own altruism and the accidents of fate.

Convincingly to anyone other than Janet, my wife, perhaps. And perhaps the police.

And myself, perhaps.

TWO

Janet disliked Peter from the start. As his interests were in quite other directions, he never really expressed any opinion of her.

I met them both at about the same time, early during my three years at Oxford. Peter attracted my attention instantly. He was charming, witty, entirely unselfconscious, impulsive in his actions, generous in his attitudes. At least he seemed so to some of us. The sight of his slightly-over-long, over-thin figure, hands and arms waving in a graceful semaphore, was enough to make us smile with pleasure.

But to others he seemed like 'a third rate actor cocking-up the role of Shelley'. I forget whether the words were Janet's, but the attitude certainly was.

My relationship with Janet took much longer to develop. At first she seemed merely a pleasant enough girl, rather vain, capable of being amusingly bitchy about most of her fellows; a not uncommon type in university life. It was a chance meeting during my first summer vacation that started our relationship. It took place, by one of life's little ironies, in the town towards which the police-car was now bearing my reluctant body, Keswick.

I had known vaguely that Jan was a Cumbrian. She had often made us all scream with laughter as she enacted in an almost incomprehensibly broad dialect 'typical' scenes of rural life, involving incest, witch-burning, or the pursuit of sheep.

Here, far from all the pressure of her position as a college wit, she was very different. I was on holiday, touring with my father for a couple of weeks before going off to France with Peter and some others for the rest of the vacation.

3

She obviously envied my money, or rather my father's. I gave her a lift home at the end of a very pleasant afternoon. She lived in a tiny village some distance to the north. At first she seemed reluctant to invite me into the small, not very picturesque cottage outside which we stopped. But when her father came to the door and stared at us suspiciously and with open curiosity, she introduced me.

He was a farm labourer, utterly content with his lot, but by no means a stupid or uneducated man. He questioned me closely about myself and my background, demonstrating an acuteness of mind and economy of language which I recognized in a more sophisticated form in his daughter.

Jan, who usually delighted to shock, was obviously very distressed by his uninhibited curiosity. I got up to go.

'Have you bedded her?' he asked casually, jerking his head at his daughter.

'No!' I denied with undue emphasis.

'Aye, well,' he said. 'She needs it.'

This became a catch-phrase for us later, but then it obviously was not in the least comic to her. This was the source of the tension between them. As far as old Will was concerned, women were created only to look after men. His wife, Mary, was perfect in this role, a bright-eyed determined little woman who watched over the needs of her husband with desperate care. A strong-minded school staff had got Jan to where she was, but her father continued to treat her as he would any woman, that is, he acknowledged domestic and biological needs, but intellectually, spiritually, she hardly began to exist. It was the complete lack of response to her arguments, protests and outbursts that frustrated Jan the most.

'I'm sorry,' she said as I got back into the car.

'That's all right,' I said. 'Look, if you ever do need it, come to me first!'

That brought a faint smile to her face. But it was I who sought her out right at the start of next term. Some seed had been sown during those hours in Keswick and I needed her.

We were married two years later after we had finished with Oxford. Peter was best man. She refused to be married in her parish church. 'They baptize pigs there if they're doubtful about their parentage,' she maintained. So we made do with a registry office. Mary came, but Will didn't. He sent me a letter, however, neatly penned, cordially phrased, full of advice. I didn't dare show it to Jan.

After the honeymoon, I started work in Leeds, in the Northern Area office of my father's business. We deal in stationery and associated products. We were near enough to Cumberland to make visits there fairly easy, but Jan refused. I had practically to drag her home once a year, and we never stayed there overnight.

Peter stayed on at Oxford to do some research and two years later was appointed to a lectureship in the Midlands. I saw him infrequently over the next couple of years and got the impression that he was becoming involved with some rather unsavoury people. But it seemed none of my business at the time. He came to stay with us a couple of times and would obviously have liked to come more often but Jan was still not keen, so I preserved the peace. Then my father died and we moved to London. I was so involved with gathering up the various threads of the business and steering through a series of crises which had arisen partly because of my father's death and partly coincidentally, that I hardly had any time for Jan, let alone Peter.

The next year was the hardest of my life. For Jan it must have been even harder. She had enjoyed queening it in the provinces as the boss's son's wife. Now as the boss's wife in London she found herself more and more neglected. I had little time for friendships old or new and the kind of people she met through me were business contacts only.

She began to voice her dissatisfactions, mildly enough at first I suppose (I don't recollect ever noticing) but more and more vociferously after a while. All I wanted was peace and quiet after a long hard day. I never seemed to get it. I started coming home later to avoid the rows. The rows increased proportionately in intensity. She ended up by accusing me of being worse than her father. I ended up by telling her that my sympathies were now entirely with old Will.

When Peter turned up very late one night, haggard, unshaven, with no luggage, he was at first almost a welcome diversion. But not for long.

A scandal had blown up at the University. It involved drugs and homosexuality. We never learned the full details as Peter was never wholly forthcoming about it and no court case was brought. But Peter had been emotionally involved with a young student whose 'moral tutor' he was. His parents, people of wealth and influence, had come across some letters Peter had foolishly written – 'things of charm and beauty, flowerily Elizabethan in style, almost Platonic in tone', he was able to describe them later – and this had been the first crack which brought the whole edifice tumbling down. Peter, who had been sucked into the group as much as any of the younger members, somehow became labelled the ring-leader. More distressing still, the young man concerned, probably in an effort to divert his father's wrath, confessed to far more than had ever happened and shifted the blame completely on to Peter, who was too shattered emotionally to be able to deny anything.

Also he had obviously been on some kind of drugs and was still suffering from the effect of these when he came to us, or the effect of being deprived of them.

We put him to bed. He woke up crying in the early hours of the morning. During the day, he said little, but sat staring vacantly at the window, as now he was sitting beside me in the police car. This pattern was repeated for three days, at the end of which Jan told me that either I got him out of our flat, or she went.

On our doctor's advice, he was moved into a nursing home the next day. As far as Jan was concerned, that

6

was that. I accused her of complete callousness and started visiting Peter more frequently than was strictly necessary, just to rub it in. The thing spiralled, Janet's protests plus the doctor's assurance of the beneficial effects of my visits to Peter took me to the Home nearly every night for an hour at least. Some weeks I hardly saw Jan at all. I took to sleeping in the guest room to avoid disturbing her if I arrived home very late. I was not encouraged to move out.

Finally early in the summer after Peter had spent nearly two months in the nursing home, things came to a head. He had made tremendous progress in the last fortnight and the doctor was sure he was ready to be discharged. 'He's not coming here,' said Jan flatly, unemotionally. I didn't argue.

'The best thing in the world for him,' the doctor had told me, 'would be a holiday. Fresh air. Sunshine. Lots of exercise.'

I felt like a holiday myself. I had worked too hard, too long. I don't think there was any malice in my choice of the Lake District. It was an area I was fond of, familiar with, and had seen too little of since marrying Jan.

She took it badly. I don't think she really believed I would go at first. And when I suggested she should come too, she exploded.

'You go with him,' she said after a while. 'You take him off, your precious boy-friend. I'll make my own arrangements. Don't send me any cards. I won't be here to read them.'

Sunshine, fresh air, peace and quiet suddenly seemed best of all things. I left the room without a word.

The following day Peter and I caught the train north.

THREE

The rain was beating down with tremendous violence now. The car's wipers could hardly cope. The windows steamed up. Nobody spoke. It was hard to believe we were in the same area as we had been for the past few days. Only the ease with which the earth was drinking up the downpour told of the sunshine we had enjoyed since the start of the week.

I had been beset by doubts and guilt feelings throughout the train journey, though Peter's infectious excitement and delight had helped to convince me I was doing the right thing. But once we started the holiday proper, the perfect weather and the beauty of the landscape made London and Janet seem a thousand miles away.

I had booked rooms in an hotel south of Keswick overlooking Derwentwater. Our plan was to spend a few nights there, then to move on where the fancy took us. We had come equipped for walking and our belongings were all packed into a couple of large knapsacks of rather old-fashioned design. They went well with the walking-sticks and stout brogues we affected as a corrective to the pretensions of the lederhosen-and-climbing-boots brigade.

We quickly established a pattern, walking all day, taking a packed lunch with us, and returning to the hotel for dinner, followed by an hour in the bar. It seemed impossible that anything could interrupt the perfection of the weather or the even tenor of our existence.

Nothing did until our last night at the hotel, and that was more comic than disruptive. At least so it seemed in retrospect.

We got drunk. We had no intention of doing so. It just

happened. Perhaps we were getting fitter and no longer felt the need to fall into bed well before ten.

The bar was crowded that night. The hotel itself was packed and there were also some drinkers from the youth hostel about a quarter of a mile down the road. Some of them looked very young to be there. I received a cheery wave from one blond-haired, open-faced lad of about eighteen. I recalled he and his friends had overtaken us coming down off Glaramara that afternoon. We had been resting by the track as the boys strode by, arrogant in their youthful fitness. I had to admit their shorts had certain advantages in this weather. They had obviously found us a little amusing and a line of laughter had drifted back up the fellside. At least they had had the courtesy to contain it till they were almost out of earshot.

I waved back and looked for a seat. A couple of girls stood up nearby, revealing very short shorts and these long, tanned, flawless, and somehow sexless legs that go with them.

'Are you going?' I asked politely.

One spoke to the other in a language I did not recognize. The other grinned and they moved away. I sat down and waited for Peter to fight his way from the bar with the drinks.

'Where tomorrow, b'wana?' he asked. 'I rather fancy a bit of the briny. All these mountains can press rather close.'

'All right,' I said equably. 'We'll trot along to Seathwaite, scramble up Scafell and drop down into Eskdale. There we'll catch a train to the seaside.'

'A train?' queried Peter. 'In the middle of nowhere? And what about our walking resolution?'

'This train is just like walking,' I said firmly. 'And you'll have had enough by the time we reach it. Let's have another drink.'

This time we managed to catch the eye of one of the barwaiters. He was only a youngster. To my surprise, Peter seemed to know him.

9

'Hello, Clive,' he said. 'Bring us a couple of Scotches, will you? Harry, this is Clive. He's reading Modern Languages at Bristol.'

'And when did you strike up *that* acquaintance?' I asked after the boy had left us.

'I have my methods,' he said, smiling. But I got the impression he was taking careful note of my reactions.

We sat drinking till midnight. It wasn't till I stood up that I realized how drunk I was. Peter staggered against me and giggled.

'Shall we dance?' he said.

I wasn't that drunk.

'Let's go to bed,' I answered.

'Don't rush me,' he said.

I pushed him out of the door ahead of me.

'Can I help?' asked Clive from the bar, a look of concern on his face.

'No, thanks. My God! What's that?'

It was the dinner-gong being struck with unprecedented violence. The air seemed to shake against my ear-drums.

'J. Arthur Rank presents!' cried Peter, and brought down the hammer once more.

I forget the exact content of our interview with the manager, a small, fleshy-faced man named Stirling. I remember walking side by side with Peter up towards what looked like a great poppy-field of faces, red with indignation, which peered down from the hotel's two landings.

I laughed myself to sleep.

I think our fragile state in the morning might have induced us to spend another day in Borrowdale after all, but now it seemed politic to leave. We paid our bill, shouldered our knapsacks, and strode away with great dignity. Once out of sight of the hotel, however, we laughed so much we had to sit by the roadside till we recovered.

Then we set off in real earnest, to cover as much ground as we could while the sun was still relatively low. It was obviously going to be another very hot day. Soon we had removed our jackets and tied them, rolled, to our knapsacks. After only half an hour I had suggested that we should abandon our notion of going up Scafell and should merely admire it from afar. Our plan was to go up Styhead, cut across to Sprinkling Tarn and thence via Esk Hause to drop down into Eskdale.

We stopped for a rest. Ahead towered the immense crags of Great End, above us to the right was the stony sharpness of Great Gable. We lay back and looked behind us down into Borrowdale. Far below I could see the minute figures of half a dozen other walkers. A bird sang violently overhead for a minute, then was silent.

Peter stood up and peered down the slope, shading his eyes with one of his extraordinarily large hands.

'Can't you rest?' I asked.

'No,' he said, and moved between me and the sun. For a second he seemed strangely menacing. Then quite close I heard the sound of boot on stone. Peter swung round. Approaching us were the blond-headed boy and his friends. They passed quite close.

'Hello again,' I said. 'Warm enough for you?'

'Yes indeed,' he said.

Peter said nothing and watched them out of sight. He obviously wasn't going to settle, so I stood up and put my knapsack on.

'Come on,' I said.

We didn't stop again till we reached the top of the Hause (the top, as far as we were concerned, being the lowest point at which we could cross!), where we rested again before the descent which I knew could be more strenuous than climbing up. Peter regarded it as a kind of bonus, however, and let out little cries of excitement as he rushed away in front of me, carried on by his own weight and momentum.

I shouted at him to be careful, then laughed at myself for sounding like an old woman.

11

But when he got out of sight and I hadn't caught up with him a few minutes later, I began to shout again.

'Over here,' came a voice from my left.

There was still no sign of Peter and a faint stirring of worry began in my stomach, and suddenly it churned violently as I caught sight of his knapsack, abandoned on the ground.

I ran up to it. It was near the edge of a deep, narrow, precipitous gully with a dried-up stream bed at the bottom. From about thirty feet down, Peter's face looked back up at me. For a second I thought he had fallen, but almost immediately realized what he was doing. Just below him, apparently wedged in a crack in the rock-face was a sheep, its trapped legs bent at an angle that made me sick to see. It rolled its head up at Peter and let out a rattling bleat.

'For God's sake, Peter!' I said. 'Come back up! We'll tell someone when we get down the valley.'

He looked undecided, then turned as if to start climbing. The sheep, disturbed perhaps by the movement – though I must say it looked horrifyingly like a start of protest against our leaving – twisted sharply, half freed itself and fell out-wards, its hideously broken foreleg now revealed plainly, dangling like a broken branch held only by the bark.

I turned away. When I looked back Peter was beside the animal, bending over it with a thick-bladed bowie-knife (the object of much amusement earlier) in his hand.

'For God's sake, Peter!' I called again.

'I can't just leave it!' he snarled and stabbed down. The beast struggled violently, a great spurt of blood jetted out and ran up Peter's arm, then it went dreadfully slack.

'Jesus, Jesus, Jesus,' said Peter, leaning back against the rockface and taking great gulps of air.

'Now, please, Peter, please come up.'

He turned without demur and began to climb towards me, his face white and set. Most of the strength seemed to have left his limbs and by the time he reached the slight overhang at the top of the gully, I began seriously to doubt whether he could make it without help.

I lay down, leaned forward, took one of his hands in mine and began to pull. He seemed a dead weight.

I was so immersed in what I was doing that when a voice spoke in my ear I almost let go.

'Hello,' it said. 'Want a hand?'

I turned my head and my nose almost brushed against a remarkably fine pair of breasts. Or the nearer one at least. They were covered only by a flimsy bra over which they strained voluptuously.

The girl reached over the edge of the gully and seized Peter's other hand.

'Heave ho!' she said.

Whether it was the extra pulling power of the girl's hands or the attraction of the rest of her, I don't know, but Peter popped up like a jack-in-the-box.

He sat there, getting his breath back, and I stood up to thank our helper. But surprises were not over. There were two of them. I realized at once they were the foreign girls whose seats we had taken in the bar the previous night. But their legs were no longer the eye-catching feature. Above their mini-shorts, all they wore were their bras. They had a small haversack with them and I could see their blouses tucked through the straps.

They both wore their hair long and might almost have been twins. The only instant way I saw of separating them was that Peter's saviour wore a white bra and the other a deep blue one.

I must have stared too hard at the difference for suddenly White-bra giggled and put her hands up to her breasts. She was obviously nearer sixteen than the twenty-five her figure could have claimed. I noticed with a start her right hand had blood on it. From the sheep by the way of Peter, whose left arm was caked with a dusty red.

He stood up now.

'Are you all right?' the girl asked sympathetically.

'Yes, thank you, dear,' said Peter. 'It was very gracious of you to help.'

13

He solemnly kissed her hand. White-bra giggled again and said something to Blue-bra in the language I had heard the previous night. Blue-bra giggled back.

I must have looked puzzled.

'Olga's my pen-friend, from Sweden,' White-bra explained.

'A fine country,' said Peter, who had never been anywhere near it. 'Thank you both again, for the help you have given me, and the spiritual stimulus you have given this old gentleman here.'

Well, *you're* fully recovered, I thought, and set about dragging him away before his whimsy took him too far. He saw what I was at and strode ahead with a broad grin on his face. I murmured my own thanks and set off after him. After fifty yards or so, I glanced back and waved.

They waved back, two arms over four circles; two blue, two white.

I smiled at the thought of the odd impression they must have of us, and hoped we wouldn't meet them again.

It was a hope the realization of which was never to give me any pleasure.

FOUR

We stopped twice more on our descent into Eskdale, the first
time to eat the stringy ham sandwiches Stirling had probably picked personally to go into our packed lunch. To wash
them down I had a super-sized flask which I had filled with
iced lager by courtesy of Peter's waiter. I mentioned this.

'Clive?' he said. 'That was nice of him especially when we
were in such disgrace.'

We laughed once more at the memory. Peter seemed
to have recovered completely from the episode with the
sheep.

Our second halt was in the valley. We had diverted
slightly to have a look at Cam Spout as it poured down
from Mickledore and had followed the stream down to Esk
Falls where it mingled with another which came trickling
down from Bowfell. Here the track levelled out and we were
able to take our ease after the exertions of the steep descent.
Eventually we reached a spot where the waters broadened
into a pool about a dozen feet across. Peter decided he
wanted to bathe. There was no one around, but I don't
think it would have mattered if there had been. Quite
unselfconsciously he took off his clothes and stepped in.

'Come on in,' he said. 'The water's lovely.'

Prudence, or prudery, made me hesitate a moment. Then
my clothes were off and I leapt in beside him.

Peter flung a handful of water at me with a laugh and
next minute we were engaged in a splashing match which
soon degenerated into a wrestling match. Eventually, half
drowned, we relaxed again and let the sun warm all that
was uncovered by the water. My eyes were closed, but
suddenly I sensed a shadow on my skin and looking up

I saw a man standing on the bank. He was dressed for walking and looked an imposing figure as he tood there, my angle of view making him seem taller than he was. His broad sunburnt face and thick grey-red beard added to the general impression of forcefulness and power. I was sure I had seen him before.

'Good day to you,' he said with a slight Scottish accent. 'If I wasn't so modest, I'd join you.'

'Please do,' I replied.

'No, no.' He grinned. 'I'm getting old. I couldn't stand the comparison. Good day.'

So saying, he touched his stick to the floppy hat he wore and strode away down the track.

Shortly after this, we clambered out and dressed ourselves. I noticed Peter did not put back on the shirt with the blood-stained sleeve, but replaced it by another.

It was only a few miles now to the village of Boot. There was a fairly large inn nearby with hotel pretensions in the summer. We were both now feeling very tired.

'If,' I said, 'if they can fit us in, I suggest we leave the seaside till tomorrow. It won't go away.'

By luck, there was a double room available, a cancellation, almost a miracle at this time of year, the manager assured us. An expensive miracle, it appeared when we enquired the cost. But I hadn't got the will-power to go any further now.

We were shown upstairs to our room and I collapsed on the nearest bed and closed my eyes for a couple of seconds. Or so I thought.

When I woke Peter was standing over me dressed in his 'respectable' kit.

'Come on,' he said, 'or we'll miss dinner. I've been down already and it smells gorgeous.'

'Borrowdale seems a million years ago,' I commented as I sipped a well-diluted scotch in the bar.

'Yes, doesn't it? I bet it's raining in Seathwaite.'

16

An anxious little waiter stuck his head round the bar door and waved at Peter.

'Jesus,' I said, 'do you always make friends with the most unimportant members of the domestic staff?'

'That,' he said, 'is Marco. He is Italian. He is here for the season. He is telling me that if we really want our dinner, we'd better get a move on or else the chef, a man with a vicious tongue and I suspect a gangrene on his shin will run amuck. I have ordered for you.'

We went in. Nearly everybody else was at the pudding stage. Over in a corner with a rather pretty young girl was the bearded man who had passed us as we bathed. His semi-formal attire made him look even more distinguished but older too. He must have been well over fifty at least.

He had his back to us but to my surprise the girl on seeing us enter reached over and touched his arm and he turned to look.

With the attractive smile I had remarked earlier, he waved genially, then returned to his food. The girl watched us to our seats, though not blatantly.

The mystery was explained when we sat down.

'That,' said Peter, with a flicker of his left cheek muscle in the direction of the bearded man, 'is Richard Ferguson, the bird-man. With him is Annie Ferguson, the bird.'

'His wife?'

'His daughter, you fool. It's no use looking for reassurance that your advancing years have not put you on the shelf. They're v. devoted, almost incestuously so. His wife, I believe, is an invalid. Might even be dead.'

I had heard of Richard Ferguson, had even listened to a radio talk of his on one occasion when I had been too comfortable to reach out of my bath to change the station on my transistor. He was much sought after, so I gathered, as a broadcasting pundit. Some accident of chance had led the BBC to adopt him as one of their panel game and quiz team 'characters'. It seemed almost incidental now that he was also one of the country's leading ornithologists.

'How did you meet him?' I asked.

'Introduced myself in the bar. When a man's seen you naked, you've taken the first step to friendship after all.'

'From the way his daughter's looking at us, he's obviously described the scene to her too.'

'Well, it's too good a tale not to be retold.'

Our soup arrived in the slim brown hands of Marco. I ate with gusto.

Peter's suggestion that we had a couple of drinks in the bar after dinner I firmly refused. I left him there and watched the telly for a while, struck up a conversation with a couple from London, read half a page of the *Daily Telegraph*, then went to bed.

It had been a splendid day. I had a self-congratulatory sense of physical achievement. I was well fed, pleasantly sleepy and lay in a comfortable bed. To cap it all, a large yellow moon shone right outside my window. I saluted it and fell asleep.

I don't know what time Peter came up but when the knock came at our door in the morning he was already up and dressed. He looked pale and told me as we went down to breakfast that he was suffering from sunburn as a result of our bathing party the day before.

'I can't walk today,' he said. 'I doubt if I'll ever walk again.'

Marco's smiling greetings had gone almost unacknowledged and the little Italian did not look at all happy when he brought us our bacon and eggs.

'Not to worry,' I grinned. 'Today we go by train.'

Marco slammed Peter's plate down in front of him. His thumb was in the fringe of the egg. As he removed his hand the egg came with it, then sliding free, it fell towards Peter's lap. Peter with the casual rightness so hated by Jan lifted the edge of the tablecloth and caught the greasy object. He looked expressionlessly at Marco, then spoke.

'Marco, can't you organize something that makes sense out of this chaos?'

Marco's underlip suddenly shot out and he began to gabble in Italian, lowly at first, but soon swelling in volume till everyone in the room was looking at us. Ferguson and his daughter, I noticed, had just come in and were standing by the door openly observing the scene with great interest.

Marco reached some kind of climax and halted. I thought of applauding, but a look at his face made me think again. He was very angry. Peter still sat there holding the tablecloth like a bridal train.

Ferguson moved over to us and spoke sharply in Italian. Marco caught the remnants of the egg up in his hand, flung it on to the plate and strode away to the kitchen.

'Thank you,' said Peter, releasing the tablecloth and standing up, partly to avoid the last oozings of the egg yolk, partly in acknowledgment of Miss Ferguson who was hovering behind her father. 'That was kind. May I introduce my friend, Harry Bentink.'

'Hello, Bentink. We have met in a manner of speaking. And I heard a great deal about you last night.'

'How do you do,' I said, half standing up with a bit of fried bread impaled on my fork which I waved nonchalantly at the girl. The bread fell on to the table.

'You're not having much luck with this table, are you?' said Ferguson. 'Come and share ours.'

He did not stay for an answer but moved across to the corner where he had been sitting the night before. We followed.

'My daughter, Annie,' he said. The girl smiled politely but said nothing. I got the impression she was scrutinizing me very closely behind her impassive façade.

'Are you here on holiday or business?' I asked.

'Bit of both,' he said. 'Never know what you'll see on the mountains.'

'That's true,' said Peter in what I recognized as his facetious tone. 'We saw a blue and a white tit only yesterday, didn't we, Harry?'

He kicked my leg gleefully under the table. I lashed back

and caught the girl's ankle. She drew away in greater unease than I felt the situation warranted.

'Sorry,' I said.

'That's all right,' she said. 'Will you excuse me?'

She rose and left. She'd only had a thimbleful of grapefruit juice. I let my practised eye recreate the limbs under the skirt as I watched her go through the door and smiled approvingly.

She did not come back and we finished the meal practically in silence.

Replete, Ferguson folded his napkin neatly, looked at each of us in turn and asked, 'What are your plans today?'

'We're going to see the sea,' said Peter. 'But first we're going on a mysterious train journey.'

Ferguson laughed.

'Oh, Lile Rattie,' he said.

'What?' said Peter.

'The miniature railway. It's great fun if the weather's fine. And it runs to time.'

Peter looked across at me and raised his eye-brows apologetically at having spoilt my surprise. I grinned back and looked suggestively at my watch. He nodded.

'Well, Mr Ferguson, thank you for the use of your table. We must be off, however, while the day is young.'

We all stood up and shook hands.

'Enjoy yourselves,' said Ferguson.

'You too.'

As we went out of the dining-room I looked at Peter curiously.

'Why didn't you answer Marco?' I knew he spoke excellent Italian.

He shrugged.

'He was just being rude.'

'What did Ferguson say to him, then?'

Peter laughed.

'He told him to bugger off or risk losing his unmentionables!'

Half an hour later we were striding down the road into the railway station. More than a station, it is a terminus and the incongruity of both setting and proportion have always endeared the place to me. Peter looked without comment at the narrow track and the low platform. There were not many people around at this time of the morning, I mean not many waiting to catch the train to Ravenglass, though when the train itself arrived it was quite full of trippers and hikers. They got out and dispersed. We put our knapsacks in one of the tiny open compartments and walked up the track to inspect the locomotive. Peter examined everything very closely, full of amused delight.

'It's marvellous, isn't it?' he said. 'It's not an intrusion into the place. Not like all those bloody motor-cars you find parked all over the place. You could run up Helvellyn in something like this and even Wordsworth wouldn't object.'

The exhilaration of feeling the rush of air on your face, of being able literally to lean out and pick flowers as you pass is almost indescribable. Perhaps the sense of inhabiting in reality for a while the imaginative world of childhood has something to do with it. Certainly the (so it seemed) inevitable sun, the royal blue sky, the smell of things growing, to which the occasional whiff of steam or smoke seemed a natural addition, all these contributed to the enchantment of the moment. Peter looked like a child on a perfect birthday.

'Thalatta, thalatta,' he murmured softly to himself, eyes straining ahead to take everything in. 'Soon we will see the sea.'

I nodded happily, acquiescingly. Soon we would see the sea.

Beckfoot came and went. Then Eskdale Green, Irton Road and the descent down the flank of a wooded fell to Muncaster. All too soon it seemed our journey was over and the sturdy little engine pulled us round an easy bend into the Ravenglass terminus.

I sat back for a few seconds, reluctant to move. But Peter was already on his feet.

'Come on,' he said. 'I can smell it.'

'All right.' I took my knapsack and we walked slowly up to the small booking-kiosk and the exit.

There were two men standing by the gate. They were dressed in rather shabby grey suits cut in a style that was archaic by London standards and must have been a bit behind the times even for Ravenglass.

One was reading a newspaper. The other, a smaller, altogether less restful-looking man, registered our approach and touched his companion on the arm. I was reminded of the Fergusons when we came into dinner the previous night.

The larger man glanced up, folded his newspaper into a squat little packet and thrust it into his jacket pocket. The anxious little man was already heading towards us. The big man strolled in his wake.

'Not more waiters, I hope,' I said to Peter.

He laughed. 'Not mine if they are.'

It was obvious that the men were heading for us. There hadn't been many people on the train and most of those had already disappeared.

'I think they are policemen,' said Peter.

I felt a sudden panic. To intercept us on holiday like this meant something pretty urgent. Something at the office? Hardly. A fire at home? Something happened to Jan?

'Mr Bentink? Mr Thorne? We are police officers, I am Detective-Constable Armstrong and this is Detective-Constable Lazonby.'

Peter and I nodded inanely. For a moment, overlaying worry, came the thought of how amusing it would be if we all shook hands and then went our separate ways. But only for a moment.

'We wonder if you would mind helping us in some enquiries we are making.'

'Certainly, if I can,' said I, my relief that none of my

22

personal fears seemed to be realized making me more enthusiastic than I normally am in my dealings with the police.

'Thank you, sir,' said little Armstrong. 'Then if you'd come this way. We have a car.'

'Wait a minute,' I said. 'Can't we chat here just as easily as in a car?'

Armstrong stood on his toes in his anxiety.

'I wasn't thinking of talking in the car, Mr Bentink.'

'No,' said Lazonby in a much less conciliatory tone. 'We'd like you to come to the station.'

I didn't like the sound of that, but what followed I liked even less.

'In Keswick,' added Armstrong with reluctant honesty.

'Keswick!' Peter screeched.

'Yes, sir,' said Armstrong. I found to my surprise we were moving quite rapidly towards the car-park.

'Detective-Superintendent Melton would like you to assist him with an enquiry he is in charge of.'

Superintendent. I knew enough to know this meant it wasn't trivial.

'Look here,' I said. 'Just what is this case, and how can we help?'

Armstrong looked at Lazonby with dog-like appeal.

'Detective-Superintendent Melton is in charge of the investigation into the deaths of Miss Olga Lindstrom and Miss Sarah Herbert. He thinks you may be able to help him with his enquiries,' recited Lazonby.

'Which girls? Oh, not *those* girls – the Swedish pen friend and – but how did they die? An accident on the fells?'

'Accident?' said Lazonby. 'If you can strangle somebody by accident, and rape them by accident, then it might be a bloody accident. Come on.'

Stunned, we followed. A few minutes later we were in a police car on the road to Keswick.

Some time later as the car began to labour up into the fells we thought we had turned our backs on, it began to rain.

23

FIVE

We had been driving for more than half an hour before I summoned up courage to speak. I prefaced it with an offer of cigarettes. Lazonby accepted.

With an effort to sound casual (an effort all the harder because of my sense of how stupid it was that I should have to try at all) I asked, 'What exactly happened to the girls?'

Lazonby took so long in replying that I thought he was just going to ignore the question. But finally he said, 'Exactly, we don't know. But we will know, eventually. At the moment all we know is that some time last night they were raped. Then strangled. Then thrown in a gully. Probably in that order. That's all we know.'

He looked me full in the face.

'But it's enough to be going on with, don't you think, Mr Bentink?'

I nodded foolishly and decided to try to turn the conversation yet again.

'What kind of man is Mr Melton?' I asked.

Lazonby thought a long time about this too.

'He's a good policeman. Oh yes. He's a good policeman,' was all that he said in the end.

But now we were fast approaching Keswick. The rain was still beating down on the windscreen almost too hard for the wipers to clean a space, but Armstrong kept his foot down on the accelerator. This seemed rather out of character for so nervous a man, but I caught him glancing at his watch, and guessed that some kind of deadline was involved. I was recovered sufficiently to be able to smile wryly at the thought of deadlines in a murder case.

My new complacency was shattered, however, as we

pulled into the small courtyard of the Keswick police station. Despite the rain, a small crowd had gathered there and as I got out of the car, I was horrified to hear from two or three throats a low baying noise, half growl, half boo, which rose in volume as Lazonby seized me by the arm and hustled me into the building.

I wrenched my arm away from him and asked in some anger, 'What do you think you're doing? And what was all that din about?'

Lazonby looked apologetic, or at least as apologetic as his solid impassive face permitted.

'I'm sorry, Mr Bentink, but you always get a funny type of person hanging around the station on cases like this. They want a glimpse of the murderer. I had to rush you in. There was a photographer there, and I'm sure you didn't want your picture in the papers, did you?'

'Why no,' I said, still feeling uneasy about the whole incident. I looked around.

We were standing in a kind of foyer about twelve feet square. There was a counter running the length of it, topped by frosted glass with a couple of compartments in it, like the windows of a railway booking office. One of these was open and through it two uniformed policemen eyed us with undisguised interest. The door which led through this partition into the office behind it opened and a sergeant came out. Armstrong stepped forward and spoke to him. He nodded and disappeared again.

'Won't keep you a moment,' said Armstrong brightly, obviously pleased at the prospect of getting rid of us.

I turned to Peter. He had slumped down on to the bench which ran along the wall opposite the partition. He looked, I thought with horror, the picture of guilt overtaken by conscience. But before I could think what to do to rearrange this allegorical picture, a door opened at the far end of the room and through it came Marco.

He stopped dead when he saw Peter. I might not have been there. Then he set off for the exit door and I thought

25

he was going to rush through it without a word. But he stopped with his hand on the knob, turned and looked down at Peter who stared back with no discernible emotion on his face, then cried:

'Pardon me, Peter. I was so angry.' This was followed by a few sentences in very rapid and emotional Italian, then he flung open the door and rushed out.

Peter, with one of those rapid transitions of mood which I realized I had noticed previously but which only now began to cause me some unease, looked up at me and winked. I glanced round quickly to see if anyone had noticed. The two constables behind the counter were chatting away to each other with great verve, Lazonby was staring thoughtfully at the door which was just swinging slowly shut on its spring. Armstrong was looking to the other end of the room where in the open doorway through which Marco had appeared stood a new figure. He was looking straight at Peter.

Something told me immediately this was Melton. Yet he looked nothing like my mental picture of the man. Perhaps I had been conditioned by television, but I had expected a large man, solid, impassive and like Lazonby except larger and cleverer. But this man was nothing like that. Short, thin, wearing an ill-fitting blue suit and, most unsuitably in every sense of the word, a green and orange checked waist-coat, he had a triangular face swelling from a narrow chin to broad expanse of forehead, accentuated by a far-receded hairline. He wore spectacles, round, cheap-framed, with bi-focal lenses.

He stepped into the room.

'Emotional creatures, these foreigners, aren't they? Mr Bentink? Mr Thorne? Thought I had you spotted. Yes, emotional. Easily upset. Show it all. Not like you and me, Mr Thorne, eh?'

His voice was high-pitched, but perfectly controlled, lacking entirely the over-rapid pace and near squeakiness of the normal high male tone.

'It's good of you to come. I'm Detective-Superintendent

26

Melton. We'll try not to keep you any longer than is necessary. Though on a day like this you might as well be here as anywhere, eh?'

'It was sunny in Ravenglass,' said Peter in a childishly sullen kind of voice.

'Yes, yes. I dare say it was. Come along now.'

He turned and walked back through the door. We followed him into a long corridor with several doors leading off. One of these was open and sitting behind a desk there was a figure cast much more in the mould I had expected. He was a big solid man, about sixteen stones of him I reckoned; he made Lazonby seem a puny youth.

'Ah, Inspector Copley. Just the man. I wonder if you would have a chat with Mr Thorne here and take his statement. In you go, Mr Thorne.'

'Aren't you coming too, Harry?' asked Peter appealingly. I could see signs of strain on his face like those which had seemed permanently etched there during the first weeks after his breakdown.

'Mr Bentink will come with me,' said Melton politely but firmly. 'We'll get things done much more quickly that way. We don't want to keep you hanging about, do we?'

He turned away, but Peter still stood in the doorway, his hand tightening on the jamb till his knuckles whitened.

'I don't see how we can help anyway,' he said in a high, strained voice, looking straight at me. 'We only saw the girls once, in the hotel bar. We never saw them again.'

His gaze fixed on me for a few moments longer, then he turned into the room and the door closed behind him.

I stood in bewilderment. What Peter meant by his last comment seemed clear enough to me. He wanted me to enter into conspiracy with him to conceal our second meeting with the girls. But why should he want this? Why?

'Come along, please, Mr Bentink,' said Melton. 'Let's see if we can find somewhere to stow ourselves.'

He led the way further down the corridor and stopped at the last door.

'Here we are. This will do, I think.'

He opened the door and waved me in. I stepped forward, then stopped dead. Sitting there reading a large type-written sheet was Ferguson. He looked up.

'Hello, Bentink,' he said.

'How on earth did you get here?' I asked.

He grinned.

'Our policemen are wonderful,' he said.

'I *am* sorry,' said Melton. 'Come along, Mr Bentink. We must obviously look further afield.'

We turned the corner at the end of the corridor and went up a flight of stairs. Up here we were obviously on a different plane of existence. There was a carpet on the floor, not luxurious but sufficient, and the room he finally took me into was very different from the bare functional boxes I had had a glimpse of below. Again, it was not luxurious, but it was reasonably spacious and the emulsioned walls looked bright and fresh. The furniture just consisted of a large desk and three or four chairs, but even these looked solid and reasonably expensive compared with the flimsy hardboard affairs below. And the room's biggest advantage was that it had a real window. I went to it and peered out. The rain was slackening off a bit it seemed and visibility had improved, but it was hard to believe in the brilliant sunshine of the previous day.

Melton had come to stand beside me and he seemed to catch the tail-end of my thought and take it further.

'If it had been like this yesterday, those girls might still be alive.'

We stood in silence after that looking out on the rain-washed landscape.

The police station was a fairly new building situated on the outskirts of the town and it backed on to some open fields which stretched away to the near fell-slopes. As I looked up at the dimly discernible heights, I felt I could imagine all kinds of sinister and dreadful happenings taking place there, but not what had happened the day before.

28

That seemed somehow too urban, native to those stretches of heath or parkland which pass for the countryside near large towns rather than this wilderness whose terrors were not made by man.

'Shall we proceed now, Mr Bentink?'

I shook off my mood of abstraction and took the proffered chair. Melton smiled at me, placed the fingertips of his hands carefully against one another and stared down at the resulting pinnacle.

'Now, Mr Bentink,' he said. 'What can you tell me about the deaths of Miss Olga Lindstrom and Miss Sarah Herbert?'

'Absolutely nothing,' I said.

There was a long pause. I began to feel rather embarrassed for Melton, who was waggling his fingers around now as if rather uncertain how to go on.

Finally he took a deep breath and spoke.

'Obviously I did not get you to come all this way, at considerable expense to the taxpayer, just so that you could tell me absolutely nothing.'

'Obviously,' I agreed.

'Then why did I fetch you?' he asked.

'You tell me,' I said.

'No,' he said. 'You tell me. You did come, after all. Voluntarily. Why did you come?'

'Why, to help you with your enquiries.' I cursed myself for mouthing the well-worn phrase. He smiled.

'And did you feel you could help?'

'No,' I began, but was quickly interrupted.

'Then I am indeed grateful that you've come all this way despite your conviction that your journey was useless. That was very good of you.'

I began to grow angry.

'Look, Superintendent, if you want to translate co-operation with the police as a confession of guilt, that's your business.'

Again he interrupted me.

'Forgive me, Mr Bentink. I was just interested to know

29

if there was anything relevant to the case which you felt you yourself would like to mention. That's all. We don't encourage amateur detectives but the ideas of intelligent men, especially those who have been on the spot at important times, are never ignored by us. I'm sorry you feel suspicious of my motives. All I want is information. All the information. All the little bits you might have stored away, quite unknown to your conscious mind. I set no traps. I just want to help you remember.'

'Remember *what*?'

'If I knew that, I would not need to trouble you any further. Perhaps a little confirmation to start with. You are Henry Aldgate Bentink of Flat 67, Montagu House, W.C.1?'

'Yes.'

'Splendid. It's not often that people are so precise or legible in their entries in hotel registers.'

'A mark in my favour?'

'It depends where in your scale of values you put precision and legibility, Mr Bentink. You are at present on a walking holiday with Peter Charles Thorne, you arrived at the Derwent Hotel last Monday evening and stayed there till Wednesday, that is yesterday morning?'

'Yes.'

'Why?'

'Why what?'

'Why did you stay there till yesterday morning, rather than, say, this morning? Or tomorrow morning?'

I did not understand his motives for this line of questioning and this worried me. What on earth could the length of our stay at the Derwent have to do with the case? I decided to be as unforthcoming as I could till he had revealed his hand.

'No reason in particular.'

Melton stood up and took a turn round the room.

'Mr Bentink, I take it you are an intelligent man, probably a University man.'

'Yes.'

'One of the penalties of intelligence is the difficulty of simulating unintelligence. It is so incongruous. Why will you not attempt to be frank with me? Either it was part of your overall holiday plan or it was an improvisation, a whim, a decision taken at the hotel. Whatever it was, there was a reason. No one suggests it was a *sinister* reason. Ninety-nine per cent of the people I talk to look for sinister reasons for all my questions when there are usually none. I know what it feels like. But let me repeat, I set no traps.'

He sat down again and looked at me almost pleadingly. I began to feel more at home, not because I believed a word of his protestation, but because this was a kind of tablemanship I was used to. Much of my working day was spent in just such confrontations and I mentally reviewed the list of preliminary self-questionings which I had learnt almost literally at my father's knee. The main question was usually whether to attack or defend. Or rather, *when* to attack.

Well, I did not know Melton well enough yet to decide who was stronger, but I felt reluctant to commit myself to the truth. I gather that this is a not uncommon phenomenon in criminal cases and perhaps the reason is what I felt on that day. I felt myself somehow threatened and the truth was a final and impregnable bastion of defence. I did not wish to come to it too soon. Do not think I felt any serious concern for myself. The crime was a dreadful one, but I had nothing to do with it. And I was rational enough to recognize my own irrationality. And also my one real reason for holding the superintendent at arm's length. This was my ignorance of what Peter was saying downstairs. He had implied that he was going to claim we had only seen the girls once, very briefly, in the hotel bar. Why?

'Well, Mr Bentink. The hotel,' he said gently.

He must know why we left when we did. He must have talked to Stirling and everyone else at the hotel. Questions about guests, time of alibis, recent departures.

31

I could not see any harm in his knowing, or anyone's knowing, as long as Peter was telling it too. And there was no reason why he should not be.

'We decided to leave yesterday morning because we thought we'd head across to the coast and spend some of this fine weather by the sea. We had decided this the previous night, but there was an unfortunate incident during the night which, though it did not make up our minds for us, certainly prevented us from changing them. But that can have no bearing on the case.'

'I gather Mr Stirling was not amused.'

'You knew,' I said accusingly.

'Ah yes. But you knew I knew. What interests me is why you bothered to work it out. Do you often get as drunk as that, Mr Bentink?'

'Not often.'

'Had you been celebrating anything special?'

'No.'

'I see.'

The stress was on the 'I'. He took off his spectacles and rubbed them on his sleeve. Then put them back on and looked at an open file which lay on the desk before him. What the hell could *he* need time to think about, I wondered.

'It was during this celebration that you exchanged words with the deceased girls, I believe. Would you tell me about that.'

'It was nothing really. I just asked them if they were coming back to their seats or leaving. They didn't reply, just jabbered away to each other in Swedish, then off they went.'

'Nothing else?'

'No.'

'Do you speak Swedish? Could you understand what they said?'

'No. No.'

'But you knew it was Swedish?'

32

'Well no. It sounded vaguely Scandinavian, if you know what I mean. And they looked Swedish.'

'I see. Did you see them again?'

This was the crunch. I postponed the moment of positive decision by attempting to imply rather than state outright that I had not seen them ever again.

'They left immediately and to the best of my knowledge never came near the hotel again.'

I thought I had got away with it, then cursed him as, appearing to want something to say rather than an answer, he repeated, 'So you never saw them again.'

'No,' I mumbled.

My reasoning was simple. Peter wanted to be kept out of this business so much that he was prepared to lie about it. If he felt so strongly, it did not matter what the reason was. In fact, the less important the reason, the more important it seemed to support him. The doctor had said he was not ready for the kind of emotional pressure the recent past had put him under. This day had brought other pressures just as powerful to a mending mind. He felt himself threatened without reason, but the lack of reason could not be explained to him until his mind recognized the lack of threat. The sooner we got away from there the better.

I am not of the cast of mind which automatically puts personal loyalties before the public good. I am not quite sure what I would do if I discovered a close friend was a spy or a criminal. But in this instance I saw things fairly clearly. Nothing I could tell Melton about our meeting with the girls around midday could possibly throw any light on what happened to them six or seven hours later.

And in the back of my mind was the smug thought that in fact to be found out in this lie would almost redound to my credit.

But I still didn't really like it, and muttered my 'no', and was heartily glad when the superintendent seemed satisfied.

'Who else was in the bar that evening, Mr Bentink?'

'I don't know any names, I'm afraid. You see we'd only been there a day and spent most of that time out on the fells so there wasn't much time to get to know people.'

I realized I was becoming garrulous in my efforts to display my eagerness to help, and I took a deep breath.

'There were a lot of people I'd seen in the dining-room. A fat middle-aged woman with a thin grey man. I can't be more exact. He was just grey.'

He smiled and sorted out a bit of paper.

'Mr and Mrs Mannering. I have them here.'

'And there was a family – two teenage sons and their parents.'

'The Fosters.'

I screwed my eyes up in the effort to recall.

'There was a party of walkers, young lads, probably from the hostel. I remember a very blond boy.'

'Ah yes. The Wyrton Boys' Club party. We have them here.'

'The manager. Stirling, wasn't it? I think he poked his head in.'

'Hardly a very startling intrusion, I shouldn't have thought.'

'Oh. Well, that's about my limit I'm afraid.'

'Really? That's not very good, is it? I mean you said the place was absolutely crowded, so crowded that the only way to get a seat was to nip in sharply as soon as anyone showed signs of leaving.'

'I'm sorry.'

He stood up.

'Think a bit more. Some other faces might come back, I know that memory's a very odd thing. Would you excuse me a moment?'

He went out. I heard his footsteps recede down the corridor and wondered where he had gone. I toyed with images of two-way mirrors and secret peep-holes through which he could peer to see if I started rifling his desk as soon as he left. The thought amused me so I smiled and wondered what he would make of my smile. But it faded away as I thought that most probably he had gone to see how Inspector Copley was getting on with Peter. But in the end I shrugged that away too and smiled again at the thought that he had very likely just gone to the loo. He looked the kind of nervous little man whose bowels might be affected by the tension of such a responsibility as his.

But I had other things to think of, besides Melton's character, though perhaps his character played a large part in the answer to the number one question which was, why had we been brought here? The more I thought about it, the more uneasy I became, though I could not see any possible reason for uneasiness, apart from the lie about our second meeting. But that lie did not exist when we had been summoned.

It had been this discussion of the crowded bar which had suddenly brought it home forcibly to me how many people were involved. A hotelful and a hostelful, plus any casuals who had been around. The superintendent could hardly have interviewed all these. Could hardly intend interviewing all these. His men would take statements. He would sift through the statements and . . . he would want to see some people personally. But why us? Why not statements first from us?

Perhaps we were mentioned in other statements and his interest had been roused. Perhaps Stirling had indicated us as suspicious characters. The bastard! I felt I had arrived at part of the answer.

But the time factor still worried me. It was only 11:30 now. We had caught the 10 a.m. train from Boot. And had been met at 10:25. How long had Melton been on the case? There was an urgency here I did not like.

But what suspicion could attach itself to us? Could it be that Melton did not know where we had been the previous evening? But he must have checked with the Boot Inn to have been able to have Armstrong and Lazonby waiting for us at Ravenglass.

I told myself I was being too subtle about the whole thing. It probably did boil down to a matter of character in the end. Melton, nervous little Melton, must have the kind of quirk which demanded that he should put himself in personal contact with everyone on the case. Perhaps he could not delegate. Probably that was why he had had to leave me. He wanted to check up on his underlings, to see what was going on.

He would be downstairs in one of the little boxes talking perhaps to Peter.

The thought did not altogether please. But it was followed by another which pleased even less.

Or to Ferguson.

What was Ferguson's part in all this? Why was he here? The only obvious connection he had with the case was not with the girls, but with us. With Peter and myself.

His presence was now the most puzzling feature of all. But at least, I thought, whatever he said must be proof positive that we were securely ensconced in the Boot Inn the night before.

I smiled and lit a cigarette. The door opened and Melton came back in.

He sat down.

'Which route did you take yesterday morning?'

'We went down through Borrowdale and then on through Seathwaite, over Esk Hause and down into Eskdale.'

'Sounds like a stroll in the park when you say it like that.' He smiled.

'It didn't feel like it.'

'Hot were you, then?'

'That's right.'

'See many people around?'

'One or two, I suppose there were a lot around, it was such a lovely day. But there's a lot of fellside up there.'

'Did you notice anyone you knew?'

I thought for a long time. The trouble with telling a lie you don't really want to tell (which rarely happens in business) is that you feel the same distaste every time you tell it, not just the first.

'We saw the party of lads from the hostel. The ones in the hotel bar.'

'That's all?'

'Yes.'

Again I was forced into the lie positive.

There was a tap on the door and a young constable came in with two cups of coffee on a tray. He placed them on the desk and went out without a glance at me. But I felt he was making a great effort to avoid staring.

'Sugar?' asked Melton.

We sat looking at each other over the tray as we manoeuvred the implements from one to another, for all the world like two housewives taking a break from shopping.

Always pick your moment for taking the initiative very carefully, my father had told me. This seemed like it, but even as I began to speak I had a feeling that the moment had been picked for me.

'Mr Melton,' I said as I took a sip of the cloudy brown liquid in my cup, 'why, when you must have an incredible amount of work to do, are you spending so much time on someone who can help you as little as I can, who only met the girls for the briefest of moments' (the distaste again) 'and who can by no stretch of the imagination be suspect. Please don't be offended by my bluntness, but I find it curious.'

He smiled.

'Well, it's better than being told one should be out catching criminals instead of manning radar traps. But you underestimate your value to us, Mr Bentink. That's what makes police work so difficult. People don't know how much they can help. It's a kind of modesty, I suppose. But something you said there interested me, Mr Bentink. Of course you're not here as a suspect, except insofar as anyone remotely connected with the case is a suspect. But why are you so certain of your own exemption from suspicion?'

Again I found myself not altogether liking his phraseology, but I could afford to be benevolent.

'Because, as you must know, Superintendent, I was visibly in the Boot Inn from six-thirty p.m. on.'

He raised his eyebrows.

'Indeed we do know that, Mr Bentink. But I fear you are labouring under a misconception of some kind. When do you think the girls died?'

'Between seven and ten, didn't they?'

'Who told you that?'

'Why, Detective-Constable Lazonby, I think it was. He implied it anyway.'

'You must have misinterpreted him. Or he himself is misinformed.'

The fingers were now back in the steeple formation. The eyes fixed firmly on me.

'The pathologist's preliminary examination indicates the girls had been dead between eleven and fourteen hours when found. They were found at three a.m. That means, as I am sure you can work out, that they died – were murdered – between one o'clock and four o'clock yesterday afternoon. And you were on the fells then, Mr Bentink. So it's not quite such an imaginative stretch after all.'

SIX

I held the coffee cup steady at my lips for as long as I decently could and cursed the slowness of my wits. I had seen men lose fortunes on the market like this. Not fully understanding what was going on, they had clung all the more tightly to their certainties, only to sink completely when these were snatched away.

Suddenly, from being in possession of a perfect abili, I had been turned adrift on the mountainside with no one except Peter able to vouch for a single second of a single one of the three vital hours. I pulled myself up mentally. There were doubtless hundreds of people in a similar position. The area must have been swarming with walkers on a day like yesterday, I thought. Lone walkers; walkers in pairs, in threes, in fours; groups of walkers, packs of walkers, columns, battalions and regiments of walkers.

'That surprises me, Superintendent,' I said easily. 'How could such a thing happen in broad daylight on such a popular stretch of the fells?'

He looked down at his papers as though at notes. But though I had seen him toy with a pencil for a few seconds at a time, he never appeared to write anything.

'You say you only saw one group of people yourself, Mr Bentink. That must have been in seven or eight hours up there.'

'There were others in the distance.'

'Who may or may not have seen you and almost certainly woudln't if you sat down. Or lay down. Or were made to lie down.'

'But noise. Screams. On a clear day.'

'Muffled by something. A sweater. A jacket. And pressure

39

round the throat. The rape and strangulation were apparently almost simultaneous.'

I felt ill.

'But what kind of people . . . in broad daylight . . . The risk!'

Melton stood up and looked out through the rain-spattered window.

'What kind of people? No special kind. At least not special in that they are going to stand out to a casual glance. Hotblooded enough to make them ignore the risk. But coldblooded enough I suspect to make them aware how little it was. This was no prolonged passionate love-making, Mr Bentink. This was a one-minute job. And then they lay there panting hard. And the girls not panting at all. All in sixty seconds.'

I sat unable to speak, or smoke, or sip coffee.

He went on.

'Then they got up. Dragged the bodies ten, fifteen yards to a shallow gully, a dried-up stream bed. And tipped them in. No attempt was made to cover them. They just tipped them in. No one saw anything then, though as you say there were hundreds of people out walking that day. And no one came across the bodies till one of the search party found them early in the morning. No one in the hostel worried till locking-up time. Even then, they did not really start worrying. It was the finest day in living memory. The night was warm and clear. No one could be in trouble on a night like this, everyone thought. But at midnight they started wondering, at twelve-thirty they started worrying. At one they started searching. Two hours later, they found them. Quite easy, really.'

'How long have you been here?'

'They woke me up at four-thirty.'

He turned round and yawned. I looked at my watch. It was midday.

'We've done a lot since then.'

I decided the time had come to really test the situation.

40

'I'm sure you must be very tired and still extremely busy. Do you want me to make any kind of statement? If so, I'll get on with it. It won't take long – I mean, there's not a great deal I can state. But I mustn't keep you back from the job.'

He looked as if he hadn't heard a word.

'Mr Bentink, are you married?'

'Yes.'

'And Mr Thorne. Is he married?'

'No.'

'Have you been on holiday together before?'

'Well, yes. When we were undergraduates.'

'You met at University?'

'Yes.'

'But you haven't been on holiday together since then?'

'No.'

'Not, in fact, since you got married?'

'No.'

'Any special reason why you came this year?'

Again I was faced with a choice. Again I tried to sidestep it.

'No, no special reason,' I said.

If I kept everything as simple as possible perhaps we might rescue the afternoon from this nightmare.

'Mrs Bentink did not mind, then?'

'Mind what?'

'Mind losing you for a week. Or a fortnight. What is it, by the way?'

'A fortnight. Three weeks. Whatever we decide.'

'Well, that's very nice, I must say. You must be self-employed.'

'Yes.'

'What?'

'I own a business.'

'What kind?'

'A firm which deals in stationery.'

'Writing-pads and envelopes, you mean.'

'Among other things.'

'Where is Mrs Bentink?'

'At home, I suppose.'

'Suppose?'

'Well, she might be away.'

'On holiday?'

'Yes.'

'But no firm plans?'

'No.'

'Not like you.'

I was growing more and more exasperated and it was only my conviction that the meek and nervous Mr Melton was deliberately aiming at this that made me keep my temper.

'Mrs Bentink is making her own plans this year. I have made *my* own plans. I would be carrying them out were it not for this business. Couldn't we hurry it up, Superintendent? It's getting near lunch time and this mountain air gives me a splendid appetite.'

He shifted his spectacles on his nose. He used them rather like a trombone player uses his slide, to get different tones. He now looked apologetic.

'I'm very sorry, Mr Bentink. It is getting on, isn't it? You mustn't miss your lunch. We have quite a good canteen here. I'll ring down and ask them to bring something up.'

I was genuinely surprised.

'I'm sorry, but I don't want to lunch here, thank you very much.'

'You mean, you want to leave.'

'Exactly.'

'But I'm not finished yet, Mr Bentink. There's a great deal more. Of course, I can't stop you leaving. You must do as you think best. But I would much appreciate an opportunity of continuing our talk later on.'

I was nonplussed. The trouble with the police, I thought rather bitterly, is that they are right and we are wrong. Melton pressed his advantage.

'I feel I should warn you that there's quite a considerable

42

crowd outside the station. Reporters, photographers, workers with nothing better to do in their lunch-break.'

'So?'

'So anyone coming out of this building is going to be subjected to a lot of questions and photographing. These reporters are persistent. At least a couple would follow you to wherever you went for lunch.'

'Isn't there a back way?'

'Oh yes. But that's reserved for people we've finished with.'

He smiled.

Always be a bad loser, my father had taught me, but let your badness be concealed.

I smiled back.

'All right. You win. But if your canteen cooks like it makes coffee, I can do without it.'

He sat down, content it seemed to go on with the interrogation right away. But I had other plans.

'I've got a packed lunch from the Boot Inn. It looked rather nice. I'll settle for that, I think. It is in my knapsack.'

We had removed our knapsacks on entry into Armstrong's car, and I had noticed Lazonby had carried them into the station with him.

'I'll have it sent up,' said Melton, reaching for the phone.

'Don't bother. I feel like stretching my legs. I'll go down.'

I got up and left the room before he could reply. I clattered down the stairs and turned into the narrow corridor. A few steps brought me opposite the door through which Peter had gone. I gave a perfunctory knock and shoved it open.

Inspector Copley was sitting on the edge of the desk, one leg dangling, looking down expressionlessly at Peter, who sat on a very uncomfortable-looking chair, his head thrown back and a handkerchief clutched to his face. It was covered in blood.

My first thought was of third-degree methods, police brutality, and all the other horrors which grow up in parallel with the myth of the helpful fatherly copper. But Copley did

43

not seem at all put out by my entrance. He obviously read the accusation in my eyes, however.

'It's his nose,' he said laconically.

Peter rolled his eyes round to the door, and saw me.

'Harry,' he said, 'it's my nose again. It just started.'

Nose-bleeds had been one of the physical manifestations of Peter's nervous disturbance while he was in hospital, indeed to such an extent that he had been in need of blood transfusions at one point.

I rushed over to him. He was pale and drawn.

'For God's sake, man,' I snapped at Copley, 'can't you see he's ill?'

'It's just a bleeding nose,' said Copley evenly. 'I put a key down his back.'

'Yes, Harry,' said Peter. 'It's just my nose. Really it is, I'm all right.'

He looked up at me pleadingly.

'Inspector Copley says we won't be long now. Then we can go.'

I interpreted his glance easily. He felt the end was in sight and could hold up till then. I felt he would be better off seeing a doctor, perhaps spending a night in hospital, but I also knew that he would regard this as a defeat and instantly cease the desperate struggle he was making to remain on the surface of reality.

'All right, Peter,' I said. 'See you soon.'

As I went out of the door I bumped into Melton. He carried my knapsack.

'I got there before you after all. Here we are. I've had some tea sent up to the room we are using so you'll have something to wet your throat. I'll let you chew in peace and join you later, shall I? Do you hear that, Inspector Copley? Mr Bentink's having his lunch here; sandwiches. He doesn't trust our cooking. Perhaps Mr Thorne would like to do the same. See that he's comfortable, won't you? Come along now, Mr Bentink.'

I let myself be ushered back upstairs. Melton poured me a

cup of tea and left. I unfastened my knapsack and pulled out the grease-proof paper packet of sandwiches. Then stopped with it half way out.

Below it lay my hat, neatly spread out with the crown acting as a kind of sack or support for the sandwiches.

The thing was, however, that my hat, made out of some phenomenally efficient crush- and crease-proof material, had been rolled up into a cylinder and thrust down the side when I had packed that morning.

My belongings had been unpacked and replaced since I arrived at the station.

I went through things carefully then. Nothing was missing, but now my suspicions had been aroused, I noticed many small items which were out of place. The knapsack had undoubtedly been searched.

I sat for a long time wondering why. I suddenly began to feel that matters were leaving my control. But once again, the certainty of my innocence made me laugh mockingly at myself and my overdramatization of events. Then I ripped open the sandwich packet and began eating in case Melton should return and find me sitting there, just staring into space.

I need not have hurried, however, for it was after 2 p.m. when Melton reappeared, full of apologies.

'There's so much to do. So much. So many little things. I'm sure you find this in business too. Now, where were we?'

'I haven't known where we were for the past four hours, Superintendent.'

'Haven't you? Perhaps that explains why you have been lying to me.'

My face settled instantly into the unemotional mask I reserve for crises, but my stomach began to bubble and pop like a panful of curry. I said nothing. I wanted to know what particular lie I was being accused of before I started defending myself.

'Mr Thorne spent the three months up to a week last

Tuesday in the Sister Moss Nursing Home near Epping in Essex. This holiday you are on is intended as a kind of buffer state between the world of the Home and the world of reality. Am I right?'

'I'll have that doctor struck off.'

'I doubt it. Mrs Bentink is unobtainable at the moment, it seems. But we have it on reasonable authority that you and she parted on the worst of terms, that your friendship with Mr Thorne had long been a source of friction between you, that in fact your marriage was near breaking-point.'

I thought of a dozen worthies of both sexes and all levels who would have delighted in offering these tid-bits. It was little consolation to know that the eleven who did not get in first would be equally willing to let me know the identity of the one who did.

'It also seems that Mr Thorne is sexually abnormal.'

I smiled.

'You find it amusing, Mr Bentink?'

'I find your way of expressing things amusing. Yes, Mr Thorne is a homosexual. But so are so many people that one wonders what is normal and what is abnormal.'

'You are not homosexual yourself?'

'No.'

'But you do not regard Mr Thorne's activities as in any way deplorable?'

'No.'

'That's very liberal of you, Mr Bentink.'

'I am a very liberal person.'

'So I see. You must know, of course, that Mr Thorne made certain advances to a young waiter at the Derwent Hotel. The boy was eighteen years old. He was a first-year university student. Clever, yes, but not necessarily very mature. How liberal are you about that, Mr Bentink?'

I shrugged.

'It came to nothing.'

'No. The boy was mature. There was another student earlier on, wasn't there? How liberal were you about that?'

I did not reply.

'Then last night. Another youth. Twenty years old. Italian. Again a waiter. Did you notice anything there, Mr Bentink?'

I nodded.

'But perhaps you were not privy to the fact that last night they slept together, they indulged in what passes for sexual intercourse between such people. Your mature, intellectual friend, convalescing from a mental breakdown, and a twenty-year-old foreigner stuck in the strangest part of a strange country. How liberal are you about that, Mr Bentink? How liberal can you get!'

He cracked his hand sharply on the desk.

I viewed him warily. I felt it was important to discover exactly how much this was a genuine display of indignation, how much a carefully controlled performance to lead me – where? My main feeling in any case was one of relief. This particular lie was not too difficult to account for. In fact, its discovery seemed to offer a new line of defence, though I did not take kindly to having to recognize I was now on the defensive.

'Look, Superintendent, as far as I could see – in fact, can see – Mr Thorne's illness has got no possible bearing on the case. I wished to save him embarrassment, that's all. As it is, now you have found out, I take it that you have instructed Copley to stop badgering him?'

'Badgering? No one is badgering. Inspector Copley is questioning a member of the public who has come voluntarily to the station to assist us. That is all.'

His recent emotion had gone and he was once again the rather dry, nervous, bird-like figure I had first acknowledged. But I knew him better now. I'm not very good on first impressions and people often exist in my mind as their own caricatures long after I first meet them. But I was quickly beginning to recognise the quality of this man.

'Fair enough, Superintendent. As for Mr Thorne's sex life, I did not know things had gone as far as you say with Marco. But if anything, surely this indicates the impossibility of his

47

being connected in any way with a rape? You can't have it both ways.'

Melton smiled at my phrase. Encouraged, I pressed on.

'There's nothing illegal about Mr Thorne fancying a young man. Nor anything morally reprehensible, no more so than if you or I should cast a lecherous glance at a couple of . . .'

I let the sentence fade away, but Melton finished it for me '. . . Teenage girls. No, you're right. As long as it ends there. But your theory of sexual exclusiveness interests me. Your friend had the misfortune to fall out with young Marco. He was still very angry when we got him here and he was very ready to talk. Among other interesting things, he reported to us a rather curious remark passed by Mr Thorne as they talked, or rather as Mr Thorne indulged in a kind of meditative monologue which Marco only half heard and half understood. Mr Thorne commented that he found it a terrible physical strain to have a relationship with a woman. To make it at all viable, he needed some extraordinary or dangerous circumstance. What do you make of that?'

Frankly, I had not got the faintest idea what I should make of it. It referred to no part of Peter's experience with which I was at all concerned. I smiled in as superior a fashion as I could assume.

'Come now, Superintendent, surely a reported remark half-heard, as you yourself put it, by a fellow who doesn't speak the language so well in any case, can hardly be very important?'

'It is part of a statement taken from a voluntary witness and must carry some weight. But by itself, I admit, it is nothing.'

By itself. I did not like the sound of that. I tried to look relaxed. Christ! I thought, I should *be* relaxed. What have I got to fear?

'Just what is all this leading to?' I asked. 'Surely, let me get this straight, there is no question of Mr Thorne and myself being suspected of this crime any more than everyone else on the mountains that day is, in the most general sense, suspect?'

He did not answer me directly.

'One of the first jobs of a detective is to look for what is odd, what is not quite in the normal run of things. Detection is often merely the sum of oddities. Your names, yours and Mr Thorne's, kept cropping up in different statements. Quite innocently, I am sure. But we must look closer as you will appreciate.'

'Whose statements, for God's sake?'

He looked through his papers again.

'Mr Stirling, the manager of the Derwent Hotel . . .'

'That time-server! Hasn't anyone ever been drunk in his hotel before?'

'I suppose so. Mr John Carboy, the head waiter, remarked that he did like the way Mr Thorne interfered with the efficiency of his dining-room service by talking with apparent intimacy to Clive Broad, a waiter.'

'That's a lie!' I said hotly. 'We only had a couple of meals in the hotel and I was with Mr Thorne most of the time.'

'Possibly. Possibly. The boy himself seems to have been very impressed with your friend, flattered by his attentions, but fortunately kept him at arm's length. He states that Mr Thorne seemed very keen to meet him yesterday morning, which was his morning off after breakfast. They had made a tentative arrangement to meet, but evidently he talked to you, realized that you knew nothing about any such arrangement, and deliberately avoided you both when you set out as he did not wish to be an embarrassment. You *did* talk to him?'

'Yes.' Silly weak Peter!

'He filled a flask with iced lager for you?'

'Yes.' That didn't sound too good either.

'Did you take a lot to drink with you on the fells that day?'

'No. Of course not. I just thought that the lager would be pleasant in view of that heat.'

'No spirits?'

49

'I've told you. No!'

'Right. Let's carry on. The barman at the Derwent in his statement says he got the impression that you attempted to pick up the murdered girls last night.'

There was a pause, not so much because I was considering what he had just said, but because with every successive use of phrases like 'last night', 'yesterday morning' and so on, I had to make a progressively greater effort to assure myself that yesterday had been yesterday, the day we climbed Esk Hause and lay roasting, carefree in the sun. The rain still spattered the window-panes. Yesterday seemed as distant as London, as the office. As Jan.

I shuddered to think what Jan would make of all this. To say our marriage was at breaking-point was the hyperbole of malice; but it was stretched taut. I was not quite sure whether I wanted the tension eased by relaxation or severance, but I knew I did not want this kind of business to play any part. I hoped fervently that the reason they could not find Jan was that she had gone abroad for a holiday. Suddenly something struck me which I had noticed earlier but which my constant concern with Peter had relegated in my mind's priorities. Why should they want to speak to Jan anyway? And with this thought came a most unpleasant awareness of the vast machinery of the law shaking and sifting my life and all it contained.

'Do you not dispute the barman's statement, then?'

'What? That! Of course I do. It's utter nonsense. I explained to you exactly what happened. Surely you can see that these people are just interested in expanding their own importance? Why, the bar was so crowded that night that the barman can hardly have noticed us!'

Melton sighed, took off his glasses and fixed me with a firm but, I felt certain, unfocused stare.

'Do not try to tell me how I should look at things, Mr Bentink. Your function is to give me something to look at. All I have so far is far from easy to understand.'

'You mean being drunk? Is that all?'

'For an invalid it's a lot. But let's move on to Mr Ferguson then. He tells us that he observed you and Mr Thorne bathing naked in a stream some miles above Boot. He says he saw you wrestling together in the water. He stressed that in his opinion you *were* wrestling, not as was suggested to him, embracing. What do you think of that?'

What I really felt was anger. I felt a sense of betrayal, as if Ferguson should have been on our side, but had for some reason gone over. I shrugged.

'It is true. We *did* have a bathe. There *was* a bit of horse-play. What of it?'

'Nothing of it. He also reports a conversation he had later with Mr Thorne in the bar of the Boot Inn. In it, let me see, ah yes, in it he says that Mr Thorne talked very freely about you and stated as the motive of your trip to the Lakes that you were recuperating from some illness. He hinted that the activities of that day had done you the world of good. Miss Ferguson who was present confirms this. I take it this is a flight of fancy?'

'Of course. Mr Thorne has an odd sense of humour.'

'Mr Ferguson also reports that he intervened in a quarrel which arose between Marco, the waiter, and Mr Thorne at breakfast. Marco said, in Italian which Mr Ferguson speaks fluently, that your friend was a cruel, sadistic, egotistical monster, that he had promised him friendship the night before, but now scorned him; that he had promised him money but now refused him; that he, Marco, had been led into sin against his family, his race and his religion, and all for nothing. He had started a pretty comprehensive string of threats when Mr Ferguson intervened.'

'I cannot confirm or deny that. I don't speak Italian.'

'Fair enough. Finally Mr Ferguson says that Mr Thorne later made a rather enigmatic remark about having seen a blue-tit and a white-tit on the mountains the day before. Being an ornithologist, Mr Ferguson naturally took particular note of the comment and says he did not understand it. Did *you* understand it, Mr Bentink?'

51

'Not really. As I said, he has a peculiar sense of humour.'

'I see.'

There was another long pause.

Finally I said, 'Is that it, then, Superintendent? Am I wasting my day here purely because one or two people have reported to you one or two easily explicable circumstances and events?'

Melton held up his index finger. The telephone, as if commanded, rang.

He listened carefully for a moment or two, murmured an inaudible reply and put down the receiver.

'Will you excuse me for a moment, Mr Bentink?'

'If I must.'

'I think it best.'

He went out.

I lit another cigarette and, with no one watching I allowed myself to puff away with the feverishness of the troubled mind. I looked at my watch. It was three o'clock. We had been in the station too long to be able to cling any longer to the illusion that we were merely indirect witnesses. Melton obviously had serious suspicions.

I could not see how these suspicions could possibly set into certainty; on the other hand, I could see no easy way of dissipating them. But I could see that the lie I had told about not meeting the girls again would, if discovered, be very hard to explain away. I toyed with the idea of confessing to it and winning Melton's approval for my frankness. But he would see as clearly as I did that this was a confession only circumstance would have forced from me, and value it accordingly. In fact, I had a great deal to lose and nothing to gain from admitting the truth. Or so it seemed to me then. After all, I thought, the only two witnesses of our meeting are both dead.

This macabre thought displeased me so much that I stood up and wandered round the room seeking some kind of distraction.

But I was soon interrupted. The door opened behind me

52

and I turned expecting to see Melton. Instead, Copley came in, stood there looking at me with what seemed real menace in his stance and gaze.

'Ah, Inspector,' I said, 'are you finished with Mr Thorne?'

He backheeled the door shut with a crash.

'Not yet.'

'Where is the superintendent?'

'Sit down,' he said.

'I said, where is the superintendent?'

He came forward, put his right hand on my shoulder and thrust me most vigorously into the chair behind me. I tried to get up again but his hand in my chest prevented me.

'What in the hell do you think you're doing?' I finally managed to snarl through my indignation. 'I demand to see Mr Melton. I will not be treated like this.'

'Shut up, Bentink,' he said. 'Let's have a man to man talk.'

'Fetch the superintendent.'

He smiled, showing two rows of great yellow teeth.

'You'd like that, wouldn't you? They all like to talk to the superintendent. He's sympathetic. He's fair. He's so bloody fond of underdogs, he'll end up getting shagged in the street. But I'm different. Very different.'

I was seething with anger, but my reason began to get control and I recalled all I'd ever read about interrogation technique. The alternation of sympathy and aggression in the persons of two different questioners was one of the first principles as I recalled, and I told myself I must regard Copley with the same suspicion as I had Melton. But I still felt a pang of fear as I looked up at this thick-set, muscular figure which loomed over me like a mountain peak.

'I'll tell you what, Bentink,' he said, 'I've been talking to that fancy friend of yours for several hours now. He gets upset easily, doesn't he? And I've heard a lot of interesting things.'

I leapt up now and faced him.

'What have you done to him? Where is he?'

He stood only a foot away from me and smiled into my face.

'You do get worried about him, don't you? You're very protective. Like a mother hen with her chicks. Or a young lad with his girl.'

I looked at him with contempt.

'I don't have to listen to you. I'm going.'

I turned to the door, but my arm was gripped from behind and I was dragged back into the centre of the room.

'I'll have you in court for this, Copley!' I cried as he released me and took a position between me and the door. 'I'll have you in your own jail.'

'You will? You think you've got rights, don't you, Bentink? You think you're entitled to the same treatment as an innocent man.'

'What do you mean?'

'Here's what I mean. I think you're guilty, Bentink. In fact I *know* you're guilty. You're a rapist, Bentink, and a strangler, Bentink. You and your fancy boy, both.'

I stood speechless. Would he dare say this unless he believed it?

He answered as if he had read my thoughts.

'I haven't come up here to question you. I've just come to tell you. I know. We've got enough evidence on you even if you never open your mouth again.'

He stood there menacingly triumphant. I collected my wits. This must be a try-on. They had gone further than I would have believed they dared. But it could only be a try-on.

Shaken, but certain, I composed my features, essayed a smile, and said, 'Surely you should be charging me then, not acting in this ludicrous manner?'

I felt he would have hit me then had not the door opened and Melton came in.

He took in the scene at a glance and motioned with his head to the door. Copley went out without a word.

'Superintendent, I wish to protest about the behaviour of

that officer. He has manhandled me and used threatening and abusive language.'

'Really?' said Melton. 'I'm surprised. Inspector Copley is an extremely enthusiastic and energetic policeman, but he never oversteps the mark. What did he say exactly?'

'Say! He said that I was guilty of this crime, he said that there was a homosexual relationship between Mr Thorne and myself. He even said he had enough evidence to get a conviction at this moment! Do you consider statements like this over-stepping the mark or not?'

I brought my fist down on the desk in an imitation of Melton's own earlier gesture. I had been uncertain of his own sincerity then, but I myself was passionately sincere.

He let a silence grow between us until the muscles of my face began to ache slightly at holding their expression of anger.

Then he said, 'Inspector Copley's fault as I see it has been anticipatory rather than slanderous in nature.'

Again a silence. The implications of his remark sank slowly in.

'After all, Mr Bentink, he has not said a single thing, it seems, which I do not believe to be true.'

SEVEN

I think that if I had been guilty this is the point at which I would have confessed. Copley's violence was nothing beside the quiet certainty of this man.

'I didn't do it,' I found myself saying. 'But I didn't do it.'

'Mr Bentink,' he said softly, 'is there anything in your story you would like to change? Or anything you would like to add?'

I looked at him wretchedly, my mind still telling me it could be a trap. Like coming in and saying your accomplice had confessed. I said nothing.

'Mr Bentink, I have a statement here from Mr Samuel Cooper of the Wyrton Boys Club, supported in all essentials by five other members of the Club. Mr Cooper states that yesterday he and his friends were on the fells and they saw you and Mr Thorne twice. Once at the time and place you yourself described. The second time, later. From a greater distance. He says he saw Mr Thorne and yourself talking to Miss Lindstrom and Miss Herbert.'

'At how much greater a distance?' I asked dully.

'About a quarter of a mile.'

I looked up.

'But one of the party had a pair of binoculars. It was through these that you were seen.'

I reached forward and put my hands on the edge of the desk.

'All right. I lied. We did meet the girls. But remember I lied before I knew the significance of the time.'

He leaned back and looked up at the trap-door above his head.

'Indeed I will. I find it very interesting that you lied

56

before you were certain that *we* knew the significance of the time.'

'One lie's not enough to arrest me on, is it, Superintendent?'

'Of course not. We usually reckon on at least one major lie per witness, innocent or guilty. But there are other things. There's Mr Thorne's shirt, for instance.'

'His shirt.'

'Yes. Among other things his friend, Marco, told us, one we found very interesting was that Mr Thorne asked him to get rid of a shirt. He gave it to him all bundled up and, in fact, asked him to burn it. Fortunately the heating of the hotel is done by electricity, so it was impossible for Marco to do this. So he just thrust it into one of the dustbins outside the kitchen. Where we found it. It was soaked in blood.'

I was aghast for a moment. Why the introduction of a blood-stained shirt should make the case against us more certain, I could not tell, but the very *idea* of bloodstains seemed damning. But I quickly recovered.

'But that was sheep's blood, Inspector. Surely your labs can tell you that? And in any case the girls were strangled. No one said anything about blood.'

'Very true,' said Melton. 'And of course our labs did tell us it was only sheep-blood. Though how his shirt came to be covered in sheep-blood is interesting in itself. But I am quite prepared to believe that Mr Thorne's motive in giving the shirt to Marco was merely to dispose of an item of clothing which by accident had become distastefully stained. If it had been more sinister, he would have got rid of it himself.'

'Well then,' I said, part triumphant, part bewildered.

'I have just received another lab report,' he said. 'A rather curious one, they thought. In cases like this, everything is checked very carefully of course. And traces of blood were found on Miss Herbert's hand, and on her bra. Sheep's blood.'

I remembered White-bra's half-pleased embarrassment

as I stared at her breasts and the way she had raised her hand to cover them.

'But that's where we met them. Just after Mr Thorne's shirt got stained.'

'What a pity you hadn't told us this earlier. It would have sounded so much more convincing.'

I couldn't help agreeing with him.

'In any case, how did Mr Thorne come to be stained with sheep's blood?'

I was so concerned with this new turn of events that I answered over-casually.

'He cut its throat.'

Then seeing his face, I hastened to add, 'It was dying, in pain, trapped on the rock-face.'

'So he cut its throat?'

'Yes.'

'I see.'

There was a fastidious note in his voice which I did not think was assumed.

'The girls helped him.'

'To cut its throat?'

'No. To get back to the top. That's when Miss Herbert must have got the blood on her hand.'

'And on her bra? How did it get on her bra? There was none on her blouse.'

'She wasn't wearing a blouse. Just a bra.'

'You surprise me.'

'It was the heat,' I said desperately. 'They had taken their blouses off just as we'd taken off our jackets.'

'So you found yourself alone on a sunny fell-side with two extremely attractive and half-naked girls?'

'You might put it like that.'

'Is there any other way of putting it? What happened then?'

'Nothing. We went on our way.'

'Saying nothing? Without comment?'

'Of course not. We thanked them. Then left.'

58

'That's how it happened?'

'Yes.'

'Allow me to suggest another possible train of events.'

He adjusted himself in his chair, arranged his fingers in the now familiar structure, coughed gently and began.

'You, a thirty-three-year-old businessman having grave difficulties with a crumbling marriage, and Mr Thorne, a thirty-two-year-old teacher, who left a university post because of a homosexual relationship which developed with one of his pupils and who has spent the past three months in an asylum recovering from a breakdown, you two have come on holiday to the Lake District. Your clothes and your behaviour draw attention to yourself. It's almost as if you are expressing some kind of intellectual scorn of the plane of existence on which most people move. Mr Thorne is quite blatant in his own sexual oddities and you yourself seem to tolerate if not participate in these. You romp with him, you share a bedroom with him, you bathe naked with him, in a manner which can only be described as exhibitionistic. You meet these two girls in the bar. You personally display considerable interest. Your friend, whose tastes are manifestly different, less. But when you meet them again, half-clad, the following day, Mr Thorne perhaps aroused already by his slaughter of the sheep, perhaps stimulated by the danger of the situation, danger which he tells Marco that same night he needs to make a relationship with a woman possible, is as eager as you are to get his hands on these girls. They, however, are not co-operative. Willing to flirt, perhaps, but no more. You want more. It is very difficult for one man to rape a woman without first inducing at least partial unconsciousness. Perhaps this is all you intend. But you go too far. Finished, you drag their bodies to the nearest place of concealment, roll them in, then continue on your way. And a few hours later you can take a bath in public with every sign of merriment.'

'Slim evidence,' I managed to say.

59

'Perhaps so, Bentink. But there is something more. Your friend, your accomplice, Thorne, has confessed.'

As I have indicated, if they had tried this one earlier, I would have been very ready for them, but now it was believable. Anything was believable. It was with no emotion at all that I saw Melton stand up and I waited for him to recite the formula of the charge which television again has made so familiar to all of us. But if that was his intention, he never started it. From below there came an ear-piercing scream followed by a confused babble of voices. It sounded as if a small riot had broken out. I found out later that what happened was that Sarah's parents had arrived at the police station. They had been taken there after identifying the bodies. As they were being led along the corridor below, Peter had been brought out of the room where Copley had been interviewing him.

Mrs Herbert had already heard that the police thought they had the men. Now face to face with this guilty-looking figure, her control snapped and she flew at him screaming and tried to drive her nails into his eyes. A constable who seized her by the shoulders was savagely punched by her husband. Even Copley got involved in the fray.

Melton rushed to the door and flung it open.

'What the hell's going on?' snarled Melton at the man outside with more passion than I thought him capable of.

'I don't know, sir,' said the constable, stiffly at attention.

'Watch him,' snapped Melton, jerking his head at me. Then he strode away down the stairs.

I am not a man of action. Normal emergencies make me become more static than ever. I liked to weigh all the facts before acting. Jan despised me for it, said that if I caught her with another man, I'd need a board meeting before I'd decide what to do. She might have been right. But now I did not make a decision. I just acted.

I kicked that poor policeman in the stomach as he came through the door, then brought both my fists down on his shoulders as he doubled up.

The result was not quite what it usually is on the pictures. Firstly, he did not collapse unconscious on the floor but knelt there making violent and nauseating gurgling sounds. Secondly, I felt as if I'd broken my wrists.

The constable was trying to get up so I thrust him with my foot out into the corridor where he hit the wall with a great thump and slid down it in a most cinematic way.

I closed the door, jammed a chair against it, seized my knapsack and rushed over to the window.

It was so stiff I thought it must be somehow locked. I put my shoulder to it but the only result was that I cracked one of the large panes of glass. Finally I sat on the desk and attacked it with the sole of my shoe. The congealed paint which held it shut gave way suddenly and it swung open, letting in a blast of sodden air.

There was still no sound at the door behind me. Some concern for the man outside made me pause a second. But the very recollection that I had attacked him was incentive enough to drive me on. I slung my knapsack over my shoulder, lowered myself to the full stretch of my arms from the window-sill, and dropped to the yard below.

I landed awkwardly and my heart pumped so hard, I thought it would drive the blood through my ear-drums.

But with a resilience I did not know I possessed, I was up in a flash and over the small wall at the back. There I crouched in the wet grass, the rain still blowing hard down from the fells. I peered into the drizzle. That at least would give me shelter from pursuit, but what I soon would need was shelter from the rain.

I was not sure why I had escaped, but I was determined that I was not going to be brought back like a drowned rat after only a couple of hours' freedom.

But I had to get away from the vicinity of the station. As yet all the activity was still confined indoors. But any second they would be outside looking for me.

I scrambled along on all fours, following the wall. After about fifty yards it stopped and became a hedge. I peered through. I had left the station area behind and was now at the back of one of the neighbouring private houses. It looked deserted.

I reached into my knapsack, pulled out my hat and my plastic raincoat, and put both of them on. Then I forced my way through the hedge and stood in the middle of a small vegetable garden at the bottom of a long lawn.

I set off at once bearing to the left to put the garage between me and the house, but stumbled on a bed of onions and fell flat on my face. At that moment the back door opened and a woman came out. I lay very still, but she was in too much of a hurry to avoid the rain to look towards me, and dashed into the garage. A car started up. I waited till it had left the drive before standing up again, an onion in my hand. I was about to throw it away when suddenly I had an idea. If I was to be on the run, I would need food. I looked around, and twenty seconds later had a couple of onions, a bunch of carrots and also some runner beans stuffed into my knapsack. Then I set off up the lawn, along the drive and out of the front gate, into the road.

Now I was faced with a very important decision. I could turn right and move out of the town, along the road which eventually would take me back to the Derwent Hotel and Borrowdale. Or I could move into Keswick itself. This road would take me back past the police station. Indeed I could see the crowd standing outside the station all staring with great interest at the blank face of the building.

Neither alternative had much appeal. But I certainly didn't want to go anywhere near the Derwent. In any case, they would have their cars out along the roads in no time and I would be a sitting duck. On the other hand, to walk back down to the station, though it was the kind of boldness which always paid off in fiction, did not attract me much either.

My mind was made up by two things. A police car pulled out of the station yard and turned in my direction and a little knot of walkers, looking like some strange religious order in their dripping oilskin capes, came trudging along from the other direction.

I tried to give the impression I was sheltering in the lea of the hedge, and as they passed I tagged on at the back, my head down, hat pulled low against the rain. The police-car accelerated by and disappeared from view, but I was now firmly committed to moving back into the town.

The walkers I was following stopped when they reached the crowd outside the station.

'What's going on?' asked one of my adoptive companions of a bystander.

'I'm not sure. They've got those fellows who murdered those girls in there. And everyone seems to be running around like mad.'

'Perhaps they're preparing the rack and the iron-maiden,' said a wag.

'That's what they need,' said an elderly man who I felt sure wore a boyscout's uniform under his riding mac.

The teenagers in the vicinity looked at him with interest.

'You'd like that then would you, dad?' asked a rather dirty-looking girl.

The scoutmaster did not reply, but turned away, calling, 'To me, Twenty-Third Troop. On parade,' and several young boys detached themselves reluctantly from the crowd.

I complimented myself on my powers of observation, then cursed myself for my lack of them as I suddenly became aware of Copley standing in the front yard of the police station slowly scanning the crowd. I crouched down and began adjusting my shoe-lace. When I peered forward again, he was gone.

The rain suddenly came down harder with that personal vindictiveness only rain in the Lakes seems to have. The onlookers began to disperse except for the hard-core of sensation-seekers, the same semi-circle of emotionless faces you see outside 10 Downing Street, at times of crisis; at the gates of the famous who were dying, being born or getting married; peering greedy-eyed at celebrities, at street-accidents, at fires, floods, and the scenes of murders. They remained as anonymous and as interchangeable as film-extras.

Before moving off I paused for a moment as an interesting thought struck me. Perhaps the real murderers were standing there, blank-faced, rain-swept, their bodies under their passive oilskins racked with unimaginable emotions. So powerful was this impression that I almost turned back, but the urge to survival was at the moment greater than the desire for vindication.

So I drifted away, trying to look as if I was attached to one group or another, but as we got nearer the centre of town, they were nearly all siphoned off by the shelter of cafés or souvenir shops. I strode on doggedly through the down-pour, knowing I had to get out of Keswick before Melton finally decided he had better plug up the town. But when I turned into the street where the bus-station was situated, I knew I was too late. A policeman stood there, talking to two young men and looking at something they were holding out to him. It could only be some form of identification. He nodded, then replaced whatever it was – driving licence, library ticket, letter – in their wallets, and went on towards the buses, laughing to each other.

I shrank back into a doorway. At first I gave Melton credit for super quick thinking, but I quickly realized that this check had probably been going on all day. Here and elsewhere. It was probably intended as a frightener. It frightened me. I waited till the constable turned away and slipped back quickly into the main street. It would be pointless trying the railway station. That would be covered also. The rain was bouncing up off the pavement like hail-stones, a small gale was whistling along the street about knee-height, I was hot and sticky under my badly ventilated mac.

Jesus! I thought. And I'm innocent. Why on earth should I run? And had it not been somehow that I could not bear the thought of being stared at from those dull grey faces,

I think I would have turned there and then and made my way back to the police-station.

As it was I was so dejected and disorientated that at the next street intersection I stepped heedlessly off the kerb almost into the path of a large car.

It squealed to a stop, the window was wound down, a face peered out and a voice said, 'Mr Bentink?'

I stood and looked down silently, prepared for re-arrest or rather arrest, as technically I had not been arrested yet. Or even charged for that matter. It was Annie Ferguson.

She looked up at me disapprovingly, as she had done in the hotel, I recalled.

'Good-day,' I said.

'You are getting wet. Can I give you a lift anywhere?' she asked with cool good breeding. I was surprised, then realized that as far as she was concerned, I was merely a recent acquaintance – not an escaped suspect in a murder case. Melton had not had time for that kind of publicity – in fact, he doubtless hoped he'd be able to avoid it.

'Thank you,' I said, and climbed in beside her. The rain ran down the crevasses and gulleys of my plastic mac and dribbled on to the thick-piled carpet. She made no comment but stared at this with some distaste. I was rather surprised. I had not imagined she was the type of girl who would put machines before men.

'I'm sorry,' I said, gesturing at the water.

She caught my meaning instantly.

'No. It's not that. I was looking at your legs.'

I glanced down, surprised, and was again surprised at what I saw. My right trouser leg had sustained a severe tear and the white flesh revealed through this was scored with a nasty-looking scratch through the congealing surface of which fresh blood still oozed.

The sight of this coupled with the luxurious padding of the seats which coaxed my body to relax suddenly made me realize what a state I was in. Both my legs were extremely sore, my left kneecap aching as much as my right calf. My wrists and forearm were very stiff and the palms of my hands were badly abraded, a fact which was partly concealed by the thick layers of mud which clung to them as it did to my shoes and the lower part of my trousers.

'What on earth have you been doing?' she asked.

'Oh I went cross country to get out of the rain,' I adlibbed furiously. 'Tumbled over a couple of times.'

'And you didn't seem to miss much of the rain either,' she said, starting the car. 'Where can I drop you?'

I indulged in a sudden fit of coughing while I thought this one out. The further away, the better, was the only real answer. But if I mentioned a distant destination, obviously she would only take me round to the bus or railway station.

'You sound as if you've caught a cold.'

In fact the cough, simulated to start with, had rapidly developed into the real thing.

'No,' I spluttered. 'I'm all right. How far are you going, Miss Ferguson?'

She looked at me curiously.

'I'm going to Cockermouth, actually.'

'Really? That would suit me fine. If you don't mind giving me such a long lift that is.'

'Not at all,' she said without enthusiasm and the car moved off. 'How were you going to get there without me? Not walk, surely?'

'Oh no. Bus. Yes, bus.'

'Really? You were walking away from the bus-station, you know.'

'Was I? I don't know Keswick very well.'

A silence followed and I grew tense as we approached the outskirts of town. If I knew my Melton he would have a road-block up before the Carlisle and Cockermouth roads separated, if he was bothering with road-blocks, that is.

He was bothering, of course. It was such a simple procedure in a town situated like Keswick. A couple of cars could plug it like a wine-cask. And I saw the car he was using to plug the North exit coming up fast behind. What had held it up, I don't know. Perhaps the policeman who manned it had been caught up in Peter's struggle. Certainly I felt that Melton would have had it in place ten minutes earlier if he had had his way.

'The floor is awfully wet,' I said, taking a duster out of the glove compartment. 'I'll mop it up, shall I?' So saying, I crouched down as low as I could get and began dabbing away at the carpet. Annie looked down in amazement at my puny efforts. I was still sufficiently awake to matters other than my own peril to remark what a very fine pair of legs she had. My only hope was that the police would not come up fast enough to overtake us, and seeing only a woman in the car, would not have any interest in any case. Whether he would have stopped us had he overtaken the car, I'll never know, for he was foolish enough to blow his horn impatiently as he came up behind and began to pull out to get by.

'Road-hog,' said Annie; a delimitation sign came into view, she put her foot on the accelerator and the powerful engine exploded into violent action. We soared away from the car behind (at least, I assume we did, for I was keeping as low as possible during all this) and a few moments later were out of danger. I sat up and looked back. The police car had stopped where the A594 curved away from the 591. As I had guessed, Melton was not using two cars where one would do. They had missed me by about five seconds.

Annie slowed down a little and smiled apologetically.

'Sorry if I bumped you, but I can't abide people who make excessive use of authority.'

She had a very pleasant Scots lilt to her voice and her face when she talked was like an illumination of her words, a kind of visual aid, animated, her meaning revealed in every feature. She sat, minute behind the wheel of the big car, but not dwarfed by it. The strength in that supple body was obviously in control of the power in that great engine.

She caught me looking at her, and her animation was

67

quickly replaced by the social mask she had adopted the previous night.

'You don't like the police then?' I said.

'I didn't say that,' she replied. Then, 'You've been at the police station today, haven't you? How did you find them?'

I was startled for a moment, but then remembered her father.

'Ah yes. I saw your father there. How did he get there so quickly? He was still in the Boot Inn when we left.'

'A policeman called soon after breakfast. He was looking for you, actually.'

Melton must have got a lot of people out of bed very early indeed, I thought, to be after us by breakfast.

'When he learned you'd gone, he made a telephone call, then started asking questions.'

'About us?'

'Oh no. About who'd been out walking the previous day, and where they'd gone, what they had seen. In the end, he asked Daddy and that little Italian waiter if they could possibly come to Keswick to see Superintendent Melton. Daddy was not very keen at first, but when he told us what it was all about, he naturally said yes. We were going on to Cockermouth to stay with friends in any case, so we just packed up and came. We even brought Marco, so the police did well out of us.'

This explained a lot. Obviously what Marco and to a lesser extent, Ferguson, had told the police at Boot had been phoned in to Melton and this is what caused the change of our plan and our own arrival at Melton's HQ. From being possible witnesses, we had become suspects. And the more they talked to Marco, the more suspicious they would be. It struck me that here was the cause of Peter's sudden desire to avoid telling the truth about meeting the girls a second time. Marco's Italian outburst at the station must have told Peter that his shirt was found, and that his relationship with Marco was known and that he was a prime suspect. Perhaps the hysterical Italian had painted things blacker than they were. Perhaps Peter, quicker than I was, had recalled that one of the girls had got blood on her. So he had decided to lie. And had warned me of his decision, certain that good old Harry would back him up.

I suddenly wondered if Melton also spoke Italian.

'Where's your friend?'

Where indeed? I thought, but answered, 'Oh, he went on ahead to book us in somewhere. There were a couple of places I wanted to have a look at, but he didn't feel up to it.'

'You must be keen in this weather.'

'Where's your father? Not still with the police surely?'

'Oh no. He was soon finished there. No one keeps Daddy longer than he feels it necessary.'

She laughed at the thought, but I smiled at the thought of even blunt, honest Ferguson, the broadcast panel's delight, getting away from Melton if he wished to keep him.

She went on, 'We had lunch with some people he knows just outside Keswick and he's stopping on there till this evening. But they're a bit old for me, really, and I did tell our friends in Cockermouth we'd be there for tea, so I've left him behind. They'll drive him over this evening.'

We had now turned off the main road and were passing through Braithwaite village. The road now began the long steep ascent up to Whinlatter pass. I settled back in my seat and pretended to be enjoying the scenery, but now for the first time since I had kicked that poor policeman in the stomach I had a moment to think. I glanced at my watch. Only twenty minutes had elapsed since I had made my break. It seemed like hours and the sunshine of the day before, already remote in the police-station, now seemed to belong to a diffcrent continent.

I spent little time analyzing why I had acted as I did. Panic, fear, the terror most of us have that the machinery of society which we control can turn on us and destroy us.

But of more concern to me was my immediate future.

I suppose I had some vague notion about proving my innocence or getting out of the country, but the immediate goal seemed to be survival in every sense of the word. I had no delusions that Melton's activities were going to be confined to Keswick and district. The whole county, and to a lesser extent at first perhaps, but becoming greater as time passed, the whole country were going to be involved. When I had been a boy, my favourite games had always involved pursuit. Not that that is anything unusual, of course. Nearly every child loves hide and seek, loves that feeling of intoxicating peril as 'it' gets nearer. But this had occupied all my youthful fantasies. I had in my mind escaped a million dangers; had faced and survived the onslaughts of the most terrible enemies, giving them the slip with consummate ease; had lived out rough in the bleakest countryside with the minimum of supplies. Left naked in the snow, I had made a bear-trap with myself as bait and killed the stunned creature with a dagger of ice, skinned it, used its fur for warmth, its flesh for food, and survived to wreak the most terrible vengeance. Dropped in the ocean, I always found a dolphin's back to climb upon. Adrift in space, I colonized planets. Snake-pits, firing-squads, gallows; secret-police, armies, alien-beings; jungles, deserts, polar wastes; all had nearly taken me, but none could quite succeed. I used to be continually surprised by the ease with which escaped prisoners were always caught and at one stage had even contemplated getting myself sent to Dartmoor so I could be the first man to get right away. The first part of this ambition at least was practically in my grasp, I thought ruefully, as I looked back at that daredevil creature of my mind. For now I was in the reality, although I was involved in nothing more immediately perilous than sitting in a large, comfortable car being driven by an attractive girl away from my pursuers. I felt sick with panic, faint with despair.

Something of this must have shown. Annie glanced at me and asked, 'Are you all right?'

'Yes, thanks. It's just this cold I'm starting.'

She reached forward and rummaged in the glove compartment.

'Try this.'

'This' was a large silver flask with her father's initials engraved on it. I opened it and sniffed, then drank deep, coughing as the whisky seized my throat.

'That's good,' I said from the bottom of my heart. 'It's pure malt, isn't it?'

'Is it? It's probably unsullied by the eyes of an exciseman if I know Daddy.'

'He seems to be a remarkable man.'

She glanced at me, then accepted the remark as the compliment I genuinely intended, and her eyes shone with pleasure.

Whoever got this girl, I thought, was going to be measured very carefully indeed against the standards of Richard Ferguson Esq.

We were almost at the top of Whinlatter now, the road was beginning to level off and some of my panic was melted away by the glow of the Scotch. I began to plan my next move when we reached Cockermouth. The word would obviously be out for me by now, but it seemed unlikely that every town in the district could afford to keep a watch on all outgoing transport. With a bit of luck I could slip out of Cockermouth, preferably by train, and head for the nearest large centre of population. Alternatively I could try to hide out somewhere in this remote countryside, but looking out of the window at the dripping, black-trunked pine trees which lined the road, I dismissed the thought. This terrain would do Melton's work for him. No, it had to be people. Cockermouth was too small. I would make for Carlisle. Even Carlisle was not exactly a bustling metropolis – a castle, a cathedral, and two traffic jams – but it was at least an important railway junction, offering a vast choice of exit routes. Yes, Carlisle it must be. I took another swig of Ferguson's whisky and complimented myself on having made the right decision when I walked into Keswick instead of out of it.

Suddenly to the purr of the engine was added a flapping, bumping noise. I sat up in alarm. Annie brought the car to a halt.

'Damn,' she said. 'It's a tyre gone. What a nuisance.'

For her it was just an inconvenience, for me the delay could be fatal. I pointed to a comparatively flat space on the other side of the road at the entrance to a Forestry Commission track.

'Pull over there,' I said. 'It will be safer.'

She did as I suggested.

'Where's your jack?' I asked.

'In the boot. I'll get it.'

She reached for the door. I put my hand on her arm.

'No,' I said, 'I'll get it. It's silly you getting wet as well. I'm soaking already.'

I could feel her arm muscles tensed like steel beneath her sleeve.

I took the car keys out of the ignition switch and got out of the car. The rain had slackened off a bit but it was still very damp. I went round to the boot and opened it.

Despite the luxurious design of the car, despite the silent engine, the polished woodwork, the grained leather, the thick-piled carpets, the overdrive, the power-assisted steering, despite all these the jack was still tucked away in a position which involved the removal of nearly all items of luggage before it became accessible. The suitcases divided themselves easily into two lots – the smart, modern, expensive ones in keeping with the car, which I took to be Annie's, and the old, battered, much be-labelled ones whose ostentatious modesty was, I thought viciously, more in keeping with Ferguson. Then I reproved myself, realizing I knew as little about the man as Annie could know about me.

Finally I got to the jack and went round to the offending rear off-side wheel.

Annie made as if to get out, opening her door as I fitted the jack.

'Don't bother,' I said. 'It's pointless getting yourself wet.'

'But the weight,' she said.

I ran my eyes over her slender body.

'There's not enough of you there to make any appreciable difference.'

She did not reply, but resumed her seat, closed the door firmly – not a slam, those doors were not built for slamming – and switched on the radio. A stream of pop music began to fall with the rain.

I returned to my work. I'm not very expert at this kind of thing and my consciousness of the importance of time made me clumsy in my eagerness. The car rocked dangerously the first time I got it lifted and I had to let it down again, re-adjust the jack and go round wedging rocks under the other wheels. The flatness of the road here was only relative.

I was very worried in case another car should come along and stop to offer help. The fewer risks of recognition I had to take, the better. Finally I got the jack perfectly positioned. I prised the hub cap off, seriously scratching the gleaming chrome in the process, removed the wheel trim and began to unscrew the holding nuts. Or at least tried to begin unscrewing them. They must have been fitted with a power-driven spanner and turned several twists past human strength. In the end I had to use my feet, bringing as much of my bodyweight as I could manage on to the protruding handle of my spanner. I could well have done with some assistance here, but even my sense of urgency could not overcome my absurd pride and make me ask Annie to help.

Finally the wheel was off, the spare removed from its equally tightly screwed bracket, the spare fitted, the nuts tightened the wrong way round, then the right way, the hub cap replaced without the wheel-trim, removed, and replaced properly; then I wearily put the removed wheel in the spare's place, let down the car on to the road, put the jack back in the boot, after removing again all the luggage which I had replaced so that it would not get wet, replaced the luggage for the second time, closed and locked the boot.

I straightened up with a groan. It had taken me more than half an hour. I was now even wetter than before and I realized as I looked down at the oil and grease which had joined the mud on my hands, much dirtier.

As I opened the passenger door, the music from the radio stopped and one of those informal, brief, hourly news-reports came on. The announcer's first words stopped me dead.

'The Lakeland Murders. A man has been arrested and charged with complicity in the murder of Miss Sarah Herbert and Miss Olga Lindstrom. Another man who was helping the police in their enquiries into the murder of the two girl walkers in Borrowdale yesterday has fled from Keswick police station after assaulting a constable. The man is Henry Bentink . . .' Here followed a description which I was pleased to hear sounded too general to be of much use; then – 'A massive search involving police from two counties, army units, and dogs, is being organized on the fells where it is suspected he is hiding.'

I reached in and snapped the radio off. Annie stared at me white-faced.

'Why don't you like me?' I asked.

'I knew that peculiar friend of yours and you were perverted,' she spat, 'but I didn't know how far it went.'

Her expressive features showed all the scorn and dislike only her passivity had revealed before.

'Afraid we'd seduce Daddy?' I asked with unnecessary crudity.

She reached for the ignition. I dangled the keys in front of her eyes, and wondered what the hell to do. My old mental hero would not have been in two minds. He would have taken control of the car, probably by tying the girl up and hiding her in the boot, and driven away feverishly smashing through any number of road-blocks before reaching safety. Or, as he got into his teens, the girl would have known instinctively he was innocent and, after a brief but passionate amorous interlude, they would have driven off together. It had been the introduction of the amorous interlude which had finally caused the death of Superboy for, with regrettable speed, these brief moments grew longer and longer till finally the adventure element disappeared altogether from my fantasies.

There was no hope of appealing to Annie Ferguson's instinctive awareness of my innocence I could tell from her face. Nor, even if I felt the inclination, did I feel strong enough to wrestle with that potentially violent little body and thrust it into the boot. I reached down and picked up my knapsack which I'd left on the floor. As I straightened up, I felt a violent blow on the back of my head. Stunned, I staggered back and sat down by the roadside feeling sick. Through water eyes I peered up and saw Annie leaning out of the window looking down at me. In her hand she clutched one of those large rubber-padded torches. She got out of the car and came and stood over me. Everything was very unsettled, like the horizon in a heat wave. I clasped my hands over the back of my head to fend off another blow.

'Are you all right?' she asked anxiously.

I looked up, surprise seeping through pain. I could see a conflict of thoughts on her face. Obviously she found the actuality of violence as little to her liking as I had done when I hit the policeman. I nodded, and was instantly sorry. She bent down and took the keys from my nerveless fingers. Then she climbed back into the car and started it up. Just before she drove off, she looked down at me again, then flung something out of the window on to the knapsack I had let fall on the road.

It was her father's flask, still half-full of whisky.

I sat nursing my pain and watched the car accelerate

away. And just before it disappeared from view, I had the small satisfaction of seeing the incompetently replaced hubcap fall off and go bounding along the road like a great silver coin till it too disappeared into the ditch.

EIGHT

It took nearly the remainder of Ferguson's whisky to get me
fit to move again. I had no idea where I was going to move
to, but I knew that it couldn't be long before Annie got to a
telephone. The gesture of leaving me the flask had not led
me to hope that she might let me have a 'fair start' or any
other sporting nonsense. It was merely a conscience-easer
for the pain she had caused me. Now, however, she would
be thinking of the pain she believed I had caused those
girls. Or at least, one of them. The other had been Peter's.
I wondered gloomily whether the charge involved them
both or allotted us one each. Presumably with the evidence
of the sheep's blood, Sarah Herbert would be marked down
to Peter, the Swedish girl to me.

I was now firmly convinced that Melton had not been
bluffing when he said that Peter had confessed. One of the
reasons for his breakdown had been his readiness to cave in
under pressure of guilt-feelings. Melton and Copley would
be experts at pressure.

Later I discovered I was right. He had confessed, but not at
the time Melton told me he had, though he was very much
broken down by then. It had been the assault by Mrs Herbert
followed immediately by the news, cleverly dramatized by
Melton, that I had run away which had finished him off. He
was by then ready to agree to anything. In fact, he was ready
to believe anything.

I surmised some of this, but then brought my fractured
thoughts to bear on the immediate problem, which was
putting as much distance as possible between myself and
this stretch of road before the police arrived. I had to
get off the road. The choice was simple, North or South.

Looking back later I saw that most things pointed me North. Reason did; it was the route to easier terrain once over the Whitlatter fells; it was also the direction which would take me towards my chosen goal of Carlisle. Superstition also; the last time I had chosen between South and North had led me into that fateful climb over into Eskdale.

But neither reason nor superstition were very strong forces in my mind at that moment. I was sitting on the north side of the road, but when I stood up, I staggered across to the other side. The ground here did not ascend immediately so steeply as it did to the north.

So naturally I went south.

This was not an area I was closely acquainted with and the driving rain, and closely-grown firs prevented me from getting any satisfactory picture of what lay ahead. At the same time I was not altogether displeased with the weather as, looking back after only fifty yards or so, I saw the road was almost invisible through the trees. A couple of minutes later and it had disappeared completely.

Soon I found I was climbing just as steeply as I would have been if I had chosen North. Eventually the fir plantation came to an end, and I lost the small protection of the trees afforded me against wind and rain. I kept on doggedly though I was very aware of the dangers of so doing in this visibility. But when after another thirty minutes I found myself up against what seemed a sheer cliff face, I knew better than to try to get up it. I shuffled slowly round to the left. When the ground beneath me turned into a narrow ledge below which was a drop almost as steep as the hill above, I went into reverse and shuffled round to my right. So careful was I this time to keep an eye on what lay below that I never saw the indentation in the rock against which I was pressed till I fell into it. I suppose you might call it a cave, but this would really be an exaggeration. It was, as I say, an indentation about two and a half feet deep and the same in width. But to me it was like a room at the Ritz. Squeezed in there, I was right out of the blast of the wind and the rain.

The heat of the previous week had not been entirely dissipated and the temperature of the rain was not unduly low. But I was beginning to feel the damp strike deep into my body and knew that the drop of temperature that would come with night could easily tip me into the Nirvana of death from exposure. Even now I knew I needed to take action before I started feeling comfortable. Quickly I removed my knapsack and opened it. I put my hand in and for a moment wondered what the hell I had got hold of. It was a large onion. It was, I thought, dinner. But what I really wanted to know was whether the waterproof guarantee I got with the knapsack was trustworthy. It was.

I sighed with relief and began stripping off my clothes. The upper part of my body wasn't bad. There had been some seepage round the neck and wrists, but the plastic raincoat was ludicrously inadequate as far as the lower half was concerned. I rather suspected I had brought Jan's by mistake. Above the knees I was soaked, below them I was liquid. I pulled a towel out and began rubbing myself violently. My enthusiasm reminded me of the scratch on my leg, but it was almost pleasant to feel the tingle of pain again. Satisfied finally, that I was as dry as I was going to get, I dug into the knapsack again and pulled out a dry pair of underpants and my 'best' trousers, the ones I wore at dinner, and put them on. My others I wrung out as best I could and hung up by jamming one of the legs into a crack in the rock.

Then I crouched down, made myself as comfortable as possible and ate an onion, washed down with the remainder of Ferguson's whisky. I thought of Annie Ferguson and the gesture, angry with herself perhaps, with which she had chucked the flask out of the car. I gingerly felt the back of my head; there was a large painful bump and a slight tackiness. I shook the last few drops of spirit on my handkerchief and gently patted the spot. It stung for a moment, but there really wasn't much whisky.

Still hungry, I nibbled at a carrot and watched the rain.

The wind had died away now and the rain fell like a bead curtain at the entrance to my refuge.

I closed my eyes for a moment. One way and another it had been a long and tiring day even though it was only about six o'clock.

When I opened them again, the rain had stopped, it was night and a nearly full moon was flooding the rock-face with light.

I was almost set fast in the position in which I had fallen asleep. Flashes of cramp shot up and down the whole length of my body as I straightened up. It took another ten minutes of rubbing and pinching to make me mobile. Then I stepped out of the 'cave' with some care. I did not really think that they would still be searching for me in the dark but this particular dark was a lot lighter than the rest of the day had been. For all I knew, of course, they might have been up here and past me hours earlier while I slept. But there was no sign of life anywhere now. I looked at my watch. It had stopped. It could have been any time at all. I glanced expertly at the moon but found the sky as enigmatic timewise as always. But the moon did offer some help with its brightness. I had no doubt that at first light, the beaters would be out again and Whinlatter would be a good point to start. So the obvious thing to do was for me to take advantage of the light and put as much ground as possible between myself and my present situation.

I folded my damp clothes and wrapped my raincoat round them. Then I concealed as best I could all traces of my presence in the 'cave.' After a last look around, I was ready to start.

The 'cliff' in the hollow of which I had been sheltering did not look half so formidable now I could see it clearly. Or perhaps I had arrived at it at the steepest section round somewhere to my left. I trekked a little further to the right, then scrambled up with no difficulty at all. My mind was clearer now than it had been earlier when I had left the road and I began to be aware where I was.

Despite the rain earlier, I had climbed a considerable way, inspired no doubt by my fear. I was quite near in fact to the summit of Grisedale Pike. I moved steadily forward, mapping out a route in my mind. I had no map with me – that was in Peter's knapsack – but I knew if I got to the top of Grisedale while the moon was shining, I would have no need of a map. Theoretically, of course, I should have been heading due south, but I knew – or rather didn't know – how many changes of direction I had made as I blundered about in the rain. At the moment all I was doing was heading uphill. I suppose I could have found north by tracking down the Pole Star. I could do this with consummate ease when pointing it out to anyone else. It had always been a good romantic ploy. But I had never been really sure that the star I was pointing at was in fact the Pole Star, and not some mere anonymous twinkler.

Surprisingly I was feeling remarkably sprightly. The night was fairly mild, my brisk pace sent the blood coursing round my veins and my recent stiffness was fading away. And I had a sense of purpose. In fact, I felt more like my superboy hero than I had done since the start of this business. Striding alone among the moonlit boulders I felt the master of all I surveyed, fully in control of my environment. But all I surveyed was the few feet in front of me over which I picked my path with considerable care. I couldn't afford to twist an ankle and the moonlight was bright, but deceptive. So I was hardly prepared for what I saw when I scrambled up the last steep section to the summit, halted, and extended my horizon.

I must in fact have more or less kept my direction for I recognized that I was facing south. Before me pale in the moonlight heaved a wild sea of hills, like a petrified stampede of vast, unknown animals. Away in the distance I could pick out the lofty outline of Scafell Pike.

It was a wild and terrible sight.

Turning eastward, aware of but not daring to look into the abrupt drop down to Coledale, I looked out over

Derwentwater to Helvellyn and Fairfield. And to the north as I continued my circle, I could see the mass of the Whinlatter fells and beyond in the distance a long scarf of whiteness which it took me several minutes to identify as the Solway Firth.

At last I was seeing the sea.

Westward I could not see so far. The near mountains blocked the view, but their very nearness was view enough. Superboy was not equipped to deal with such static violence as this.

I sat down on a boulder and forced myself back to my old limited horizons. The prospect of going further was now frightening to me, but I knew I had to do it. If I was Melton, I thought, what I would have done would have been to take a map and a pair of compasses, stick the point in at Whinlatter Pass and draw a circle showing the maximum distance I could have travelled in the time it took him to marshal his forces to this particular spot. Then I would dispose my men along the roads which came nearest to bounding the area, and sit and wait till I came down off the mountains. The best way of avoiding him would be to refuse to come down and force him to come looking for me. In this kind of hide-and-seek, the hider had all kinds of advantages. What he did not have was food, drink, warmth, shelter. I could not survive indefinitely on runner beans, onions, and carrots. So I had to go down to break through Melton's line and tonight was the best time to do it.

I studied the landscape again, this time shielding my mind as best I could against any but the most practical considerations. Roughly speaking, I felt that Melton would try to contain me within a triangle bounded by Derwentwater and Borrowdale to the East, Crummock and Buttermere to the South and West, Whinlatter to the North. Whichever direction I headed in, I would eventually come to a main road which must be crossed, and this seemed the most likely place for his men to be. But there was an awful lot of road to watch and in any case, I thought complacently, Melton does not know for certain I've gone South. He must look to the North as well.

I got to my feet and prepared to move. I had decided to head for what, if my theory were right, would be the nearest point of the triangle, to stick to the heights as far as possible, making my way along the ridge to the neighbouring peak of Whiteside. From there I would drop down towards Scalehill, cross the road and cut through between Lowes Water and Crummock into Ennerdale. I thought how Peter would have been entertained by the simple way I rattled off the names of the route in my mind. It had been one of his favourite subjects for parody. I wondered how he was spending this moonlit night and my conscience stirred at the thought that I might do him more good by attempting to offer rational refutations of the charge than by careering around over the mountains like James Bond.

But it was pointless letting this worry me now, I thought fatalistically. If the mountains wanted me to be recaptured, they would arrange it despite anything I could do. Melton was only human, him I could contend with. But there were forces greater than the police, I thought, casting a last look at the terrible view. Then I restricted my gaze once more to the few feet ahead of me and set off.

Melton, had I but known it, was more like the mountains than I imagined. That is, he had argued along the same lines as myself once the initial search inspired by Annie's report had been called off because of the weather and approach of night. But he had gone a stage further. The roads were not guarded – he had realized this was impossible. So he had divided the men available to him – a quite considerable number, for the press had seized on the story with delight and pictured me (by non-libellous implication, of course) as a kind of insatiable satyr roaming the hills to the peril of every woman within a radius of 100 miles – and established half a dozen groups prepared for instant action at key points in the area. His theory was that he did not need to look for me; that his trouble was going to be a surplus of reports

83

of sightings of me, but that with so many people on the fells at this height of the season I was bound to be spotted fairly soon.

He had started the machine. Now it could run itself till it needed to be re-programmed.

Thus it was that I crossed the road below Scalehill with a great deal of unnecessary care and got myself unnecessarily wet by wading across the River Cocker when I might just as well have used the bridge. I adopted the same method of crossing the stream which links Lowes Water and Crummock and as I dried myself and resumed my trousers I saw the first traces of the dawn in the sky.

I pressed on for another couple of miles, climbing steadily once more, then decided the time had come to look for somewhere to hide myself for the coming day. I had decided that my little stock of vegetables plus a bar of chocolate I had found in my knapsack would have to keep me victualled for one more day. But when night came on again, I would have to apply myself seriously to the business of restoring my larder.

I reckoned I was now on the lower reaches of Blake Fell, probably on that shoulder of it stretching out towards Lowes Water and known as Carling Knott. There was little cover here and looking back, I seemed to be dangerously close to Loweswater Village. But it couldn't be helped. Movement was what attracted attention in these empty spaces. I moved to my right where the terrain seemed rougher and much less attractive to walkers. Finally I came to a halt by two large boulders. The space between them seemed as good a shelter as anywhere, and nearby there was a small pool of water left by the previous day's rain which would serve me both for refreshment and for whatever ablutions I felt necessary.

With the aid of loose stones, I built a kind of wall at that end of the gap between the boulders which faced what I felt was the most likely route for any walkers on this not particularly popular section of the fells. When I was convinced that it looked as natural as possible, I set

84

about making the living-space as comfortable as I could, removing one or two large stones and using my knapsack as a cushion. Satisfied with this, I scrambled about twenty yards over the rocks and relieved myself. It was going to be a long day, I thought as I did so. It was now full daylight. I scrambled back to my shelter, wriggled in and breakfasted on the inevitable onion. Then, for the first time realizing how tired I was, I closed my eyes and fell asleep.

It was at this point I suppose that the Scoutmaster of the Twenty-Third troop, a ludicrously early riser, who had for the past half hour been watching my every movement through his war-souvenir German army binoculars, put them away in their case and left his tents (which to me were merely distant orange mushrooms by the lake) and strode off to the village to report what he had seen.

Had I been awake I still don't suppose I would have noticed him, but I would have noticed fifteen minutes later the truck which came winding down the road into the village. The men who got out of it would have been mere dots at that distance, but so many dots swarming around like ants would have drawn my attention and the rapidity with which they were drawn up and marched away out of my sight round the foot of the Knott would not have allayed my fears.

But, as the four pairs of binoculars now fixed on my 'refuge' could testify, I never moved.

But ten minutes later, I awoke. It may have been a sixth sense. Perhaps the mountain nudged me. Most likely it was just the enthusiastic efforts of a sharp piece of stone to worm its way into my buttock. But I awoke and peered out of my shelter.

The hill, which sloped away gently at first, then more steeply, in front of me was empty of life. I could tell by the shadow of the rocks that not much time had passed since I went to sleep. I peered down at the village. It looked as quiet, or dead, as unreal as ever. Everything told me of my utter isolation. Except my stomach, empty before but now full of fear.

Don't be a fool, I thought. It's only half an hour since you got here. There's danger enough without imagining it.

Again I scanned a full circuit of the horizon, this time turning and peering through the chinks in my wall.

Nothing.

I decided to placate my stomach with a piece of chocolate. It had melted in the heat of the earlier part of the week and now the silver paper was firmly cemented to the surface. I picked carefully at it, remembering the effect silver paper had on my fillings.

Clink.

It had come from behind me. I turned again and peered through the chinks. Through a chink to see a clink, I thought with assured calmness. Still there was nothing but rock and stones, then a frieze of hills against a background of light blue sky sponged with fluffy white cloud.

I suddenly had a picture in my mind of the other side of the ridge, dotted with silent men, inexorably moving forward, tensed for the final rush when they came into sight.

The picture was too vivid to smile at. Still clutching my chocolate in my hand, I wriggled out of the shelter and picked up my knapsack in the other hand. I stood for a moment, uncertain, knowing that by moving I was doing exactly what my reason had told me could be fatal. Melton would rely on my nerves giving way. I must not give way to imagined fears. I took a step back towards the shelter. It looked like a trap. I turned away. Far below a voice spoke into the mouthpiece of a walkie-talkie set.

'He's moving! Get after him!'

And with a tremendous cry and thudding and clashing of boots on rock, the line of men broke over the brow of the ridge like a tidal bore bulleting up the Severn.

There were about two dozen of them. They were soldiers, and their bayonet-charge cry froze me for a second.

The chocolate, untouched, dropped from my hand, then I turned and fled.

I set off obliquely down the side of the ridge which was too steep for a direct descent. The pursuers came pouring after me, silent now, saving their breath for the chase. I soon found I was in most danger from those at the furthest end of the line who had come over the crest some twenty yards up the ridge from my shelter. In order not to be cut off, I was forced to widen the angle of my descent and finally I realized there was nothing for it but to go straight down. The slope was very precipitous here, so much so that my eager pursuers had slowed themselves down and were approaching in short rushes from boulder to boulder, like balls coming down a pin table. A couple of those ahead had gone further down the slope and were now working their way round to get below me. In a few seconds I would be completely encircled.

I had read somewhere that the old slate-cutters of Honister used to bring their slate down the mountain in sledge-fashion. I had no slate, but I was determined to follow their example as best I could, and I thrust my knapsack between my legs, held tight on to the straps, took a short hobbling run to get up momentum, and sat down on it.

The ground was still bone hard, despite the rain, the grass sparse and shiny, the outside of my knapsack faintly polished by its waterproofing. I shot under the outstretched arms of the soldier immediately beneath me and, increasing my speed at an alarming rate, I skidded away down the slope.

What steering and braking equipment I had was only, of course, my legs, and I did not dare dig my heels in too abruptly otherwise my ankles would have snapped like match-sticks. My main fear was of colliding with one of the large boulders strewn about the slope, and I brushed against more than one. I had no time to see what was going on behind me. My only real conscious manoeuvre (evasion of rocks was instinctive) was to try once more to make my

87

descent oblique, rather than straight down, though this materially increased the danger of my capsizing.

This is what finally happened just as I thought the whole thing was becoming manageable. I bumped over a stone and was tipped over so that my slide became a roll which fortunately was interrupted after only a short distance by collision with a great boulder.

All the breath was knocked out of my body by the impact, and I lay there watching the sky and hillside still go whizzing by. But finally everything slowed down and I struggled to my knees.

Looking back I could see my route clearly marked by a trail of clothes and toilet articles. The knapsack, in shreds at my side, had been worn or ripped open and all my stuff had fallen out. What really amazed me was the distance I had come. The pursuit was far behind, which was just as well I realized, as I stood up and became aware of the new pains which had been added to my old aches. I felt as if I had cracked a couple of ribs and my left shoulder felt as if someone had hit it with a hammer.

I looked at my knapsack. At least now I had nothing to carry. I turned away and set off down the slope at a painful trot.

Looking back after a couple of minutes I realized I had no hope of beating these fellows in a straight race. They were young, obviously very fit, and were gaining on me with every stride. Somehow I had to go to earth and let them overtake me. But to do that, first I had to get out of sight.

I was now running along fairly flat ground at the foot of the shoulder, which is better geography than anatomy. The ground was rising again before me and I knew that I had to be far enough ahead of my pursuers to be able to drop out of sight as soon as I got over the approaching ridge. I summoned up my puny reserves of energy and increased my speed a fraction. I don't suppose the soldiers even noticed it. But they must have noticed how I staggered as I clawed my way up the sudden steepness of the last few yards.

To my disappointment the terrain beyond the ridge was merely a shallow basin stretching to another ridge about a hundred yards ahead. I would never make it, and the kind of hiding place I wanted was totally lacking here. But I had to make do with what there was.

I dropped down almost on all fours and scuttled across to a group of large stones on the extreme left of the basin and flung myself down among them – I had no time for anything more subtle. I buried my face in the rocky earth and tried to hold my breath, but nothing could stop those long shuddering suckings and blowings.

The soldiers breasted the rise and I suppose their very impetus and enthusiasm carried them another fifty yards or so before they realized that I could not possibly have disappeared over the next ridge so soon. All my body wanted to do was to lie there by the rocks, but my mind, working like a fury now, told me they'd be casting around for me any moment and, if I was to save myself, they had to do it on my terms.

I stood up. As I had guessed the soldiers had stopped and bunched together. They were looking around and three or four of them spotted me together. As their cry rose again, I was already moving in the terrible slow motion of complete fatigue back the way I had come.

My intention was simple. I had to repeat the trick and this time make it work. If it didn't I was caught. Up and over I went, sliding desperately down the steep slope on the other side.

I knew I could not possibly do it. There was nowhere to hide, at least nowhere within reach of my legs. I leaned back against the slope, my muscles gave up with relief and I collapsed back and lay utterly still, waiting to be captured.

I suppose it was my stillness that saved me. That and a soldier who had dropped out of the hunt, whether through fatigue, indolence or injury I never knew. But he was just disappearing over the next rise as the remaining soldiers came thundering back.

'There!' cried the leader, and off they went again, a couple of them, or so it seemed later, leaping right over me. I sat in numbed amazement watching their retreating backs, certain that they would turn any minute. Then slowly I rose, slowly I scrambled backwards up that damned slope again and, my eyes still fixed on those khaki-clad figures, slowly I sank down on the other side.

I knew just how temporary this respite was, but the renewal of hope also renewed my strength a little and I managed a steady walk for fifteen minutes before I had to stop by a small stream trickling down from the heights on my right. I drank deeply and bathed my scratches and bruises in the ice-cold water, which brought some relief though from the look of my shoulder, the worst was yet to come. Even in the fragmented mirror of the dimpling water I could see that I looked a ghastly sight. My face was unshaven and covered with scratches I could not even remember getting. The back of my head where Annie had struck me was throbbing relentlessly and, when I tried to stand up, I found myself swaying wildly and had to sit down again. I drank some more, lapping like a dog and looked at my reflection again.

'I warned you you were too old to play at Superboy,' I said.

My plight seemed hopeless. Melton would have me pin-pointed now. If he could conjure up two dozen men like that, with a little more time he could have a hundred. I had lost everything I had in my escape down the fells. All I was left with was a torn tweed jacket, my 'best' trousers – now long past their best – my shoes and socks. Even my 'stout brogues' seemed to have resigned some of their stoutness, I noticed with dismay. One of them was gashed along the side completely through the leather.

I rolled on my back and lay there trying to organize my thoughts into some kind of cogent pattern. Nothing my father had ever said seemed relevant to the present situation. Indeed that area of my life in which I was a man of action and decision, running a thriving business and turning losses into profits year after year seemed to belong to somebody else. I felt about it as the businessman in me had felt when I came across some of my old University essays on what seemed obscure and abstruse subjects. Did I once know all that? I thought in awe. How could I know it and let myself be what I am?

But in the end I had dismissed them as anthologies of plagiarism and assured myself that my present life was the only reality.

Now I saw that figure in the well-cut suit with the big desk, the big secretary (too big for Jan's liking, I recalled) and the big future, as an actor. I could never have been like that. I could never be like that again.

I stared up at the sky. The light blue had almost entirely disappeared and the fluffy white cloud, like a detergent commercial in reverse, had gone dark and grey and spread rapidly over the sky.

That's it, I thought. If the weather breaks again, I'll give myself up.

Five minutes later the weather broke again and I thanked God for it. I had got to a crouching position preparatory to another attempt to stand and looking back down the valley I saw without surprise the inevitable line of men moving slowly forward towards me. They were still too far away to have noticed me crouched as I was, but to stand up would be to invite observation. I just knelt there and, despite my recent resignation to recapture, the inevitability of it so affected me that I did not feel the first drops of rain. Then it came down in earnest, sweeping down the valley towards the searchers, who disappeared from my view within seconds.

I was soaked to the skin just as quickly, but to start with at least, the result was as invigorating as a shower bath, and I stood up and began to make my way up the valley again.

The rest of that day I can hardly remember. I kept to the low ground as far as possible, I sat huddled behind a boulder for what might have been minutes or hours, but the rain never let up and I had to set off again to keep some warmth in my body. At one point I found myself actually battling my way along a fairly fast-moving stream. I had been too wet to notice and it was only after I had stumbled and nearly drowned myself that I came to my senses. Soon after that I made my way towards what looked like a group of grey stones but which turned out to be half a dozen sheep seeking shelter in the lee of a slight declivity. With the imperturbability of their kind, they ignored me completely after a few investigatory prods to see if I was going to be a source of bread-crusts and I lay among them, my fingers dug into the fleece of the nearest, catching some of their warmth. I heard voices quite close by as I lay there, but whether it was pursuers or merely hikers, I did not know. In any case, it was immaterial, for everyone in the Lakes that day would have his eyes open for me.

Any purpose in my wanderings had long been lost. I did not know whether I had come five miles or fifty. All I did know was that after I left the sheep (had I lain there one hour or ten?) I became aware that I had reached a state where not even sitting and awaiting recapture was enough. If I was to survive, I had to go and find someone to capture me. My body was at the same time numb with cold and aching with pain and I could feel waves of fever racing through my skull.

I was back among fir trees again and I laughed hysterically at the thought that I might have wandered all the way back to Whinlatter. That at least would mean the road was near. All I would have to do was lie across it till a car pulled up. Or didn't pull up.

Surrender, surrender, surrender, was the only thought, if thought it could be called, in my mind.

So when I saw a light ahead, apparently very low down, I didn't care whether it was cast by a torch, a window, or the gates of Hell itself. I headed straight for it.

I had been coming downhill for some time now, proceeding in a series of painful rushes from one tree-trunk to the next. Now the angle of descent grew even steeper and a little rational area in my mind told me to take care, but my body was incapable of obeying mental instructions in any case. But the little rational area was not at all surprised when my feet slid away from under me and I skidded on my backside down a bank of shale into the small garden of a grey stone cottage whose windows glowed invitingly.

I got to my feet, absurdly ran my fingers through my hair to straighten it, and made my way to the door. It opened at a touch and I found myself in a small kitchen. To my right was another door under which a line of light glowed.

I pushed it open and stepped into a long low room. It was almost unfurnished, and there was nothing on the floor except for a line of disembodied heads. At the far end was a workbench cluttered up with various odds-and-ends, among which I recognized a potter's turntable and a mound of clay. In a clamp at one end of the bench was a large piece of stone rough-hewn into the shape of a skull.

And by the bench with a chisel in one hand and a mallet in the other was a woman.

She looked at me in silence and I stared back. We were both interesting sights, I for obvious reasons, she because she wore a blue nylon overall unfastened down the front to reveal she was nude underneath.

'Oh, it's you,' she said. 'You'd better come in.'

NINE

I closed the door behind me and leaned against it. She put her mallet and chisel carefully down on the bench, then placed her hands on her hips inside the overall, thus pulling it open even wider.

'Well?' she said.

'Well what?'

'When does it begin? The rape?'

She was a woman I could not have found attractive in any circumstances. She must have been about forty years old and her flesh was sagging badly. Her hair was almost the colour of tomato soup with one bright silver lock trailing over the rest like the spoor of a snail. Her face was broad and bold, like that of a prototype barmaid without the geniality. Her protruding underlip jutted like a ledge over the gentler slopes of her two chins.

Her breasts hung from her rib-cage like boxing gloves on a gym wall and her nipples were almost invisible. Her belly sagged over a thatch of hair very different in colour from that on her head. And even her legs, which were long and shapely, in their very perfection looked incongruous forking out beneath that derelict torso.

As I said, in no circumstances could I imagine myself being attracted to her. And at this particular moment not all the wiles of Cleopatra could have put the fire in my blood.

'No rape,' I said.

She came right up to me then till her face was only a few inches from mine.

'What's with you, Bentink? Choosey who we rape, are we?'

Absurdly, I found myself apologizing as if I had been mis-understood by my hostess at a party.

'No, no, it isn't that. Not at all. It's just that I'm rather tired . . .'

I stammered to a halt. She threw back her head and laughed as uninhibitedly as she dressed.

'Perhaps later then, eh? When you're better.'

I smiled weakly. She could afford to joke.

There was a telephone on the floor, I now noticed, in a far corner.

Once again I turned fatalist, once again my legs gave out. This time I knew that it would need more than the stimulus of pursuit or a shower of rain to put strength back in them. I slid slowly down the door till I sat on the floor. Then I keeled over to my left and subsided slowly on to my side. My head came down alongside one of the disembodied heads I had noticed. I recognized it. It was Ferguson, done in a blue-veined stone.

I winked a greeting, then closed my eyes. Distantly I felt a foot prod my stomach. Then a pair of hands fastened under my armpits and began to drag me across the floor.

I smiled complacently. It would take more than that to disturb my slumbers. And I sank into a mountain-haunted sleep.

I awoke under a blanket in a corner of the same room. The woman was still there chipping away at the stone in the vice. It might have been a mere couple of minutes since I had passed out and for a second I thought it was, but then the difference of light told me this was morning and a fine one. I raised myself on my elbow and realized that the tattered remains of my clothes had been removed. I was lying on two or three more blankets folded over to form an oblong.

At my movement, she turned round and glanced down at me. She was dressed as before, and the fact that her overall now had a couple of buttons fastened hardly concealed her nakedness any more efficiently. I was more self-conscious and clung tightly to my blanket as I struggled to my feet.

I felt rather feverish and my body was awash with aches and pains so that I grunted and groaned like an old man as I straightened out my limbs. The woman took a couple of steps towards me, reached out and whipped away my blanket.

'It's a bit late to be so bloody modest,' she said, looking at me appraisingly.

'Turn around.'

I was too weak to refuse. When I had completed the full circle, she said, 'Well, I've saved you from gangrene, I suppose, though you look a fine bloody sight I must say.'

I looked down at myself and realized for the first time just how many cuts, scratches and abrasions I had collected in my flight.

'I'd have put you in bed, but there's only mine and you're too bloody filthy. Go and have a shower. You stink the place up.'

She turned back to her lump of stone. I had neither the inclination nor the energy to assert myself and turned and went out through the door, leaning against the wall for support.

The cottage, I discovered, was built on a rather peculiar plan, or rather the 'modernization' of it (for economic reasons I supposed) had resulted in some peculiarities. It was a single-storey structure two-thirds of which was taken up by the room I had just come out of. The other third consisted of the kitchen through which I had entered the previous night and in which I now stood, and a bedroom which led off the kitchen also. The bedroom was almost sumptuous in its furnishings compared with the bareness of the living-room. A round bed stood in the middle of it and each of the four corners of the room was hidden, one by a full-length mirror, two by curtains which formed small wardrobe recesses and the fourth by a full-length picture which looked at first glance like a brass rubbing of an armoured knight, recumbent, with his arms crossed on his chest. But closer examination revealed that the picture was of the rear view of the knight and the arms crossed over his back obviously belonged to a woman underneath him. Even my rusty Latin was up to translating the beautifully lettered inscription . . . 'And the second thing I did on returning from the Crusade was to take my armour off . . .'

This shutting off of the corners gave the room a circular shape which was accentuated by the bed in the middle. There was a small window, uncurtained, presumably to avoid interrupting the flow of the wall, but provided with small flush shutters on the inside. I opened these and looked out.

I found myself peering down over a great stretch of black water which I did not recognize. The hills facing me on the far side looked peculiarly menacing even to my over-menaced mind. They seemed to close in to my left and even to the right where the aspect was more open the silhouette of one ridge in particular, with two vicious-looking needles protruding into the washed blue of the sky, made me shudder. I decided that this must be Ennerdale Water. Any other lake within reach of my fevered wanderings I would have recognized. This, because of its beautiful remoteness, I had never visited before. I say 'beautiful' not because I was still in a state to appreciate the aesthetic appeal of sky, hills, and water, but because here at least I was away from the mainstream of walkers, climbers and casual tourists. The cottage was about thirty yards from the lake edge. There was no sign of life anywhere.

I closed the shutters and opened the second door in the room. This led me into what had obviously once been the entrance hall to the cottage, with the kitchen straight ahead, the living-room (and probably another bedroom for I felt sure that the large room I had slept in must have been two rooms combined) and the present bedroom to the right, a simple enough plan. This small hall had now been made into a lavatory and shower. The old front door still existed, but heavily and unassailably bolted and barred, while the doors which had once existed to the kitchen and living-room had been removed and bricked in.

I turned on the shower which ran hot with commendable speed. I stepped in and let my flesh bask in the delicious and soothing heat for several minutes before seizing a lump of soap and beginning the job of removing the grime from my skin.

A quarter of an hour later I was feeling fit enough to start considering my situation again. The big enigma, of course, was just what I could expect from this woman. She could have no immediate intention of handing me over to the police otherwise she would have done it while I was asleep. On the other hand her attitude to me had not revealed any instinctive beliefs in my innocence or even any firm desire to help.

I stepped out of the shower and looked for something to dry myself with.

'Here, try this.'

She was leaning against the door looking at me without emotion. She held out to me a large towel which I used both for drying and concealing.

'It bothers you, doesn't it?' she said. 'That's a bit odd for a rapist surely.'

I didn't answer for a moment but finished off my towelling then tied the towel round my waist.

'Look,' I said, 'let's get one thing clear. I did not kill those girls. I had nothing to do with it. You're in no danger from me.'

She found this very amusing.

'It's you who's in danger, Bentink. From me. If you're so bloody innocent you won't mind me 'phoning the police.'

I moved forward, uneasy. The sleep and the shower had refreshed me, yes, but I was in no condition to start running again. After what I had been through, it seemed stupid to let a woman turn me in while I stood inactive only a yard away. I reached out my hand. She did not move. I touched her arm. She let a small breath escape through her nose. I tightened my grip. A sudden stirring of lust moved in my stomach.

The telephone rang.

I turned away, filled suddenly with horror at myself. I realized how relative a thing my innocence was. This woman, whose body seemed so unattractive a thing, had stirred me to a lust which another minute might have turned to action.

She was speaking now, coldly.

'No. I don't think I shall be back tomorrow. I'm doing some rather interesting work and I think I will stop on till it's finished. Goodbye.'

She replaced the receiver.

'My husband. I am Moira Jane Reckitt. My husband is William Reckitt. He is a physicist. He works at the Calder Hall research establishment. We have a flat which has been provided for us by the Government. We have neighbours who have been provided for us by the Government. We also have this place, which helped me survive two and a half years up here. My husband bought it so we could get away. Now I use it so that I can get away from him. That's my story, Bentink. You make an interesting change. That's why I'm reluctant to give you up.'

All of this except the last three sentences was spoken in a rapid monotone. It was only at the end that she resumed her old sardonic manner.

All I could say was, 'I didn't kill those girls.'

'Who cares?' she asked. 'Who bloody well cares whether you did or not? You're on the run, aren't you? Perfect innocence never ran away. Are you hungry?'

'Why yes.'

Why, yes indeed, I realized. I was almost starving.

'Get yourself something to eat then,' she said, and turned back to her stone.

I turned to go, but stopped and turned back, partly to assert my independence from her casual authority and partly to ask a very real question.

99

'Where are my clothes?'

'Those rags? I burnt them in the kitchen stove.'

That settled matters for the moment. I could hardly go scrambling over the fells dressed only in a bath towel.

I cooked myself a great plateful of bacon and eggs and followed it up with two tins of vegetable soup and half a loaf of bread. This finished, I made a pot of coffee, picked up two mugs and returned to the living-room.

She took the coffee without comment and went on with her work. I strolled around, looking at the heads on the floor.

There was something very powerful about the stone heads with the broad brutal scars of the chisel left so openly on them. She was less successful in clay, and her dissatisfaction seemed to have expressed itself in caricature – a nose pulled down to meet a bloated lip, an eye so deeply set that it was like a Cyclops in his cave.

'How long have you been doing this?'

'Not long.'

'Why did you start?'

'Mind your own bloody business.'

I stooped to the head of Ferguson I had noticed (I dimly recollected) the night before, and moved it over to get a better look.

To my non-expert gaze, it looked a first-class piece of work, possessing all the power of the other pieces yet with a much greater delicacy and subtlety of delineation.

'How long have you known Ferguson?'

'Long enough.'

'I think this is very good.'

No reply.

'Why is it better than the others?'

A few taps with the mallet.

'I suppose because he was better than the others.'

'Better?'

She snorted a laugh.

'I thought every man knew that the artist always sleeps with his models. It works both ways.'

I looked at the array of heads.

'Most of them,' she said.

'Have you met Ferguson's daughter?'

'What do you think?'

Once again, thoughts of Annie Ferguson made my hand stray to the back of my head and I suddenly felt rather giddy. I went over to the wall and sat down on the blanket which had acted as my mattress the previous night.

'You still tired? Go to bed.'

I looked at her uncomprehendingly for a second.

'You're clean enough now. Go to bed.'

The thought of sheets and a real mattress was so seductive that I swallowed my annoyance at her ungracious command and without another word headed for the bedroom.

It was as delightful as my mind had pictured and I sank into a sleep which even in its beginnings felt much more soothing than that of the previous night. It had been long, certainly, but just as when you have driven further than you should, the road unwinds before you all night, so the mountain tracks had been etched on my eyelids then. Now there was nothing except the darkness of silence.

When I opened my eyes again, Moira Jane was lying beside me, her belly heaving against my thigh. I tried to pretend I was still asleep and turned away, but a powerful hand turned me back.

'What's the matter?' she said. 'You want me for a character witness or something? Come on.'

Again I recognized that my absurd unreliable body was not at all loth to come on, and under Moira Jane's expert direction all signs of physical reluctance quickly disappeared.

I am not certain at what point enthusiasm becomes nymphomania, but Moira Jane certainly did not make any unreasonable physical demands on me. I stayed there for the next four nights and we never had it more than once

101

a night. I got the impression that this was just the climactic point of a daily process which started when I got up in the morning and brought a jug of coffee into the bedroom. She lay there expressionlessly but I noticed her eyes followed my every movement. I took over the kitchen and did all the cooking and washing up while she chipped away.

'When are you going to do my head?' I asked.

'You? For rapists I don't do heads. I'm going to do your crutch.'

Something in her attempts to shock reminded me of Jan. I found myself looking at her in horror at one point and thinking that this was what another ten years could make of Jan. Or perhaps it was what I could make of Jan in another ten years.

I suppose when you react so unfavourably to a person at first sight as I had to Moira Jane, further acquaintance must often improve matters a little; and I found myself regarding her, if not with affection, at least with an effort at understanding. I discovered that though in fact her husband, a man of some influence it seemed, had bought the cottage from the Forestry Commission on whose land it stood, it had been Moira's own money which had put it into its present shape. She obviously treasured the place above all else in her life.

I foolishly said to her, 'Didn't I read somewhere that they are going to raise the level of the lake and make it a reservoir? Won't that affect you?'

'Yes,' she said, in a way which invited no follow-up. So I didn't try. It was none of my business anyway, but I foresaw trouble when the time came.

More interesting to me was her relationship with Ferguson. In fact I was very interested in both members of that family in a strange mixed-up way.

Annie disliked me, despised me it seemed, and had almost cracked my skull open. Yet despite this, or perhaps because of it, I was strongly attracted to her. I had never been unfaithful to Jan (what was going on now between Moira

102

Jane and myself I just didn't count) nor even seriously contemplated it. Now, after just a couple of meetings in the most unpromising circumstances, with a girl who hated me, I found myself considering the shape of a future without Janet.

And Ferguson himself became more fascinating the more I learned about him. I had sneered at the blunt, oracular façade, but had not had much chance to see what lay beneath.

One of the things that lay beneath was a very highly sexed man.

'Have you known him long?' I asked more than once.

Sometimes she didn't bother to answer my questions at all. At best I was permitted to make the minimal break in her routines. But on this occasion she was almost talkative.

'Nearly twenty years.'

'And how long have you . . . ?'

'Been his whore? Seventeen years in October. I'll tell you the date if you like. And it's eight years since he finished with me.'

'You mean he doesn't come any more?'

'Oh yes. He still comes. I didn't finish with him, you see.'

She turned to face me.

'I didn't weather very well, did I? I was once middling to fair topped off with a great dollop of devotion. A bit of worship goes a lot further than a classical profile. But it all wore thin. And I wasn't getting any younger. So I caught poor Reckitt before it was too late.'

'Was that when it stopped with Ferguson?'

'Oh no. Not till later. But that was when hopes of an honourable settlement stopped.'

She laughed at her phrase.

'He'd promised to marry me when his wife died.'

'His wife?'

'Oh, yes. There's a wife. She's been bedridden for nearly twenty years. Bed-ridden. That's a funny word. On the point of death, too, from what he said. But it never came

103

to the point. And even if it had, it was too late then. Too late for me. There were others by then. He'd got a taste for it, I think. It can happen. I know.'

'His wife is dead now?' I asked.

'Not her. No, she'll live for bloody ever. That's why he still comes to see me. Her and his precious daughter. Plus his equally precious self-esteem. I have photos. Letters. So he comes and he sits and he talks. And I can feel him hating me all the time.'

She turned away from me again and stared at the window.

'One day I think he'll try to kill me.'

She spoke flatly, not to me but herself, and I couldn't read fear or hope or even resignation into her voice.

I left her standing there. I had been interested in Ferguson and in Moira's portrayal of him as a highly-sexed and potentially violent man.

He too had been on the fells that day last week.

But I had not wanted or expected to hear this ugly story of desire and blackmail. It sickened me and I tried to shut it out of my mind.

It says a great deal for human adaptability and very little for moral consistency that within a few days I was going to find the whole story very useful for myself.

The police came the third day I was there. She invited them into the kitchen and I sat with my ear to the bedroom door, praying that my washing up had been comprehensive enough to remove all trace of my presence. This was a return visit. She had told me that they had been a few hours before my arrival, warning her to look out and report anything strange.

'But you left the door open,' I said.

'I knew you'd come,' she said. 'I'm the seventh bastard of a seventh bastard.'

Now the police, disturbed by their failure to net me, were retracing their paths.

'No, I've seen nothing,' she said.

'I see. Still by yourself?'

'Yes.'

'I thought you'd be off on Monday? Didn't you say you were just here for the weekend?'

'I changed my mind.'

'I see. Well, be careful, ma'am. All by yourself here. I don't want to worry you, but this man could be dangerous.'

'I can be dangerous myself, Constable. Good day.'

She locked the door after him and came in to me.

'You could be dangerous,' she said.

That was the only time we broke our small sexual routine.

I wanted to find out what the papers were saying, but she refused to drive down to the village at the head of the lake and get them.

'You want them, you go and get the bloody things,' she said.

There wasn't even a radio in the house so I had no idea at all what was going on. I sat around all day reading books and magazines belonging to Moira Jane. My clothes now consisted of a pair of her pants – the least translucent I could find, but they still looked obscene – and one of her 'loose' sweaters which was a tight fit for me. I asked her if she would help me get some men's clothes. She replied coldly.

'Look, you can stay here as long as you want. You'll get food and drink, you'll get a bed, you'll get me. In return, I get you. That's all you've got to give me. You've nothing to offer which makes it worth my while to help get you out of here.'

'I'm going all the same,' I said angrily.

'Go. We've no agreement. But I warn you, once you've gone, I might use you in some other way.'

What she meant by this, I could not imagine. But the fact remained that I had to stomach my own wrath and indignation because my slim chances of getting right away were reduced to hopeless odds if I had to clothe myself as soon as I set out.

I began to invent wild schemes for stealing someone's clothes, schemes impossible not only because of the violence involved, but because the only men I ever saw were anglers from the fishing hotel Moira told me stood at the bottom of the lake, and they were merely distant figures in minute boats, sitting motionless and patiently in the middle of the water. I envied them as they moved away in the evening, visualizing the company, the conversation, the good food and friendship which awaited them.

Reckitt was a fisherman himself, it seemed. There was a rod carefully stowed away in the kitchen and in one of the midnight strolls I permitted myself to take the air, I stumbled across a cockleshell boat, pulled up on the lakeside, which he must have used. I contemplated having a row in it, but closer investigation revealed that it had been out of the water so long, the boards had warped a little in the sun and it looked most unwaterworthy. I gave up the idea and returned to the other half of my nightly ritual.

On my fifth full day there, that is the sixth after my arrival, I lay on the bed staring into space and wondering for the hundredth time what I should do. I suppose in a way I had found the escaped prisoner's ideal refuge, with food, shelter and a highly-sexed woman. But I knew that unless I decided something, events would decide it for me. I did not delude myself that Melton would remove his attention from this area. Certainly the net would be spread much wider now, but at the same time Melton would be using the reports of people like the constable who had so recently spoken to Moira Jane to narrow down the number of houses where I might conceivably be if I had not left the area. Houses unoccupied or occupied by one person only would come in for a very close scrutiny. In fact for all I knew the house was being watched already. I stirred uneasily. I had half hoped that something might have turned up in the past few days which indicated my innocence, but the policeman's warning had shattered that comforting illusion. He had spoken as if my guilt was the most certain thing on earth. I idly wondered if I could sue him for slander if I managed to prove myself innocent.

I still did not know whether Moira Jane believed me or not. Or whether she wanted to believe me or not. I ran mentally through a list of friends and business colleagues, trying to work out who would refuse to believe me guilty. Not one, I decided bitterly. And most of them would get a little thrill of pleasure, immediately and sincerely repressed perhaps, at my predicament. As for Jan, she must know by now wherever she had gone. Would she believe me innocent? Why should she? She had been ready to accuse me of sexual deviation with smaller grounds than this in Peter's case.

I sat up and looked around for something to occupy my mind. I had been right through the magazines which lay strewn around me making the bed look like the table in a dentist's waiting-room. I began to prowl around looking for fresh reading matter and pulled aside the curtains which shut off one of the corners of the room. Not having any clothes to hang up, I had never had occasion to go behind here before. A bar was fitted across the corner making a triangle with the walls and from it hung a variety of woman's clothes. I pushed them aside, idly contemplating disguising myself as a woman, a prospect made even more ludicrous than it normally would have been by the fact that, not having a razor, I had grown a stubbly beard in the last week.

My eyes lit up as my search met with unexpected success. Protruding from the pocket of Moira Jane's rain-coat I saw the familiar colour of a Penguin. I pulled it out and felt absurdly disappointed when I realized I had read it before. But as another piece of information I had registered swum up from my subconscious to my conscious mind, I flung the book aside and dragged the rain-coat off its hanger.

Underneath it was a suit of men's clothes.

Inside the collar of the jacket I found a tab with the initials W. R. It was obviously Moira Jane's husband's. The pockets were quite empty. I pulled on the trousers and felt an absurd sense of power and authority as I did so. The jacket followed and I looked at myself in the mirror. It wasn't at all a bad fit, a little small perhaps, but not ridiculously so. Even the pullover which was all I had to wear underneath did not look too out of place after I had twisted it round so that the V-neck was at the back.

Luckily Moira Jane had not committed my not-so-stout brogues to the stove, and I dragged them out from under the bed where I had put them after they had sat beneath the kitchen table throughout the policeman's visit. The leather was now terribly dry but they were better than the woman's slippers with trodden-down heels I was now wearing. I ruthlessly helped myself to three pairs of nylons, cut the feet off them with nail scissors, just above the ankles and used them as socks. The laces on my brogues had rotted away and snapped as soon as I applied pressure to them, so I used the nail scissors again to cut myself two strips of material from a black dress hanging behind the curtain. These did not look quite right, but I felt that if it got to the stage where my laces were being closely examined, I was finished anyway!

I took a last look at myself in the full-length mirror. I looked very different from the figure I normally presented to the public eye and began to feel reasonably confident of success.

Next I moved into the kitchen and helped myself to what food I could wrap up and get into my pockets without looking too bloated. From the drawer of the kitchen table I retrieved my wallet which Moira Jane had had the sense to remove before consigning my ragged jacket to the flames. It contained about ten pounds which I felt I was going to need if I was to get right away from the Lakes.

Finally I opened the living-room door and stepped inside.

Moira Jane did not turn round but continued her sculpting. She still had on the nylon overall which, despite the good

108

supply of clothing hanging in the bedroom, was the only garment I had seen her wear since I arrived.

I stood and watched her. She had started work on my head a couple of days before and it had been fascinating to see my own features begin to rise out of the stone. But now as I watched, she stopped, put down her tools, loosened the clamp, lifted out the unfinished piece and calmly dropped it with a resounding crash by the wall with the others.

'So you're going,' she said, turning round.

'Yes.'

'Goodbye.'

I took a step forward.

'Look, Moira Jane, I'd like to . . .'

'Shove off, Bentink. I'm not getting sentimental. You've been useful. You'll still be useful when you've gone.'

I turned and left, slamming the door behind me, stalked out into the open with no effort whatsoever at concealment but had gone only twenty yards or so before I cursed myself for being such a stupid arrogant fool. What if she had known about the suit all along? What if she had been insufferably rude? I owed her much.

I turned round and trotted back to the cottage and in through the still open door. At the living-room door I stopped. I could hear someone speaking inside. I turned the handle quietly and peered in.

Moira Jane was sitting on the floor with the telephone in her hand. She had taken off her overall and was squeezing her right breast till her fingers left ugly red weals.

She spoke into the phone.

'Yes. He's been here. He's assaulted me. Yes. He's gone now. I'm not sure. South along the lake, I think. Yes, I'm hurt. Please hurry.'

And as I watched she picked up her chisel and drew the sharp corner diagonally across her body from the left shoulder to the right thigh. She did it slowly and carefully and I saw the red blood start up behind it.

Then she looked up and saw me standing there. Her face

109

was as ever expressionless. She put down the phone and waited.

I closed the door gently behind me and sat down in the kitchen. I was trembling like a frightened puppy.

TEN

No noise came from the living-room and I had no intention of going back there. The question was, where did I have any intention of going? It would take the police some time to get here. The only road to the cottage twisted round through the fells behind, unmetalled for much of the way, and finally turned into the Forestry Commission track which skirted the edge of the lake.

I had all the time in the world to make good my escape up into the hills. But my whole being revolted against the thought. I could not face another game of hide-and-seek up there, even if the sun did happen to be shining at the moment. I suddenly wanted to be near buildings and people; I wanted to know what had happened to Peter. I felt the same stirrings of guilt every time I thought of him and how I had abandoned him. I wanted to be in London, to know that the city stretched for miles in all directions. I wanted to explain my innocence to Jan, to Annie Ferguson, to Melton.

But I didn't want to go to gaol.

It looked as if it would have to be the fells after all.

I stood up and pushed the chair against the wall. Something clattered to the floor. It was Reckitt's fishing rod. My mind lit up in a blinding flash of what is inspiration or lunacy depending on how things work out. I picked up the rod and headed for the shore.

Fifteen minutes later I was sitting in the cockle-shell in the middle of the lake, watching with calm patience the drift of my baitless line over the water. I paid as little attention to the two cars that bumped along the Forestry track to the cottage as I hoped they paid to me. In fact, it was not difficult to look unconcerned about the police. My main concern was much more immediate – it was to devise a way of stemming the flood pouring in through the bottom of my boat. For a wild moment, I laughed at the picture of myself sinking like Buster Keaton beneath the surface without a flicker of emotion, not daring to call for help.

There were several other boats on the lake and I wondered if anyone had remarked on my stealthy progress from the shore. There was a light haze on the water which protected me from too much attention and as the afternoon drew on the declining sun laid the black shadow of the heights to the south-west across the water. I could hardly see the cottage now. It seemed unlikely that they could have noticed me.

The water problem seemed to have solved itself, or at least disaster seemed to have been postponed. There was a good six inches of water in the boat; my behind was feeling damp and my feet were soaked, though this did not worry me too much as I felt that a bit of damp could only do good to the dried-out leather of my brogues. I reckoned that the warped planks of the boat had absorbed so much water that they had swollen back into place. Or nearly, anyway. It was probably still seeping through. The danger was going to come when I started rowing again. I noticed that at least one of the other boats was pulling away down the lake in the direction of the hotel. I had no desire to be left in splendid isolation all night.

I took off a shoe and began to bail. This was a long job as I had to do it surreptitiously in case I was observed, and by the time the boat was manoeuvrable again, the last of the real fishermen was moving off. I hastily pulled after him, noting with dismay after a few strokes that this relatively violent activity had opened up new wounds in the bottom of my boat. I decided that speed was my best bet now and threw myself at my oars like an Olympic sculler. I didn't exactly race across the water, but I had almost caught up with the last angler by the time we reached the stone wall which fronted the hotel. He turned to watch me ashore and kept a remarkably poker face as he saw the water swishing about in my cockleshell. I stood up and leapt casually on to the steps.

Behind me with a sad gurgle Reckitt's boat sank beneath the surface.

'Close,' observed the angler.

I laughed inanely.

'It adds a bit of spice to the sport, eh?'

He nodded and turned away. I quickly fell into step beside him – he was the only bit of cover I had. I felt he would be glad to shake me off, and hoped I could depend on that terrible need to be polite which is the essential creed of the English bourgeoisie.

He stopped by an Austin 1100 parked alongside the hotel.

'If you'll excuse me, I want to pop along into the village before dinner,' he said, unlocking the door.

I didn't know whether this was a real desire on his part, or merely an overcomplicated way of shaking me off. Not that it mattered; I couldn't go into the hotel alone. I couldn't really have gone into it in company, I suppose, but alone, it was out of the question.

'Why, so do I,' I said brightly. 'And I see my wife has taken the car. Could I beg a lift from you?'

What could the poor man say? He said nothing as he drove very hard along the track which led from the hotel to the road. It was quite a distance and I was glad I had not tried to walk it.

The village was quite full. It seemed as if the day's allotment of visitors had descended on it all in the same hour. From the dashboard clock I saw it just on opening time and wondered if this had anything to do with it. My driver pulled up in front of the small shop and began to get out. I toyed with the idea of remaining seated and stealing his car as soon as he was in the shop. I had almost dismissed this as foolish when he reached back in and removed

113

his keys from the ignition switch. His eyes met mine. I got out.

'Thanks a lot,' I said. 'I'll make my own way back. I can see my car up there' (I waved vaguely) 'so my wife must be around somewhere. See you at dinner, eh?'

He smiled with relief and locked the car.

'Cheerio, old man,' he said, and went into the shop.

I set off boldly down the village street luxuriating in the company of people and the noise of cars and conversation. But my boldness and my delight vaporized as I spotted a policeman's helmet making its way on a collision course towards me. A few yards ahead, set back a little from the road, was a low whitewashed building on the front of which a weathered and peeling board proclaimed that here was the Ennerdale Arms. I increased my pace, thanking heaven for the civilizedly early opening times in this part of the world.

Something rang a warning bell in my mind as I passed between the cars parked in front of the inn. Something to do with brightness. But the policeman was too close for me to stop and work it out. I pushed open the pub door and went in.

Two things happened, apparently instantaneously, but I suppose one must have preceded the other, perhaps caused the other. I realized that what I had seen outside was a large car, not uncommon in make, but somehow familiar. With one very bright and obviously new hub-cap.

And with his back to me for the moment and his head squeezed into one of those allegedly sound-proof telephone shelters which looked incongruously modern in this ancient building, there was the bird man of Boot, Richard Ferguson, hardly a yard away.

I turned.

The policeman was leaning up against Ferguson's car, mopping his brow.

Ferguson seemed to be speaking angrily into the phone. I suddenly knew with absolute certainty that he had rung

Moira Jane's cottage. And was probably talking to the police.

There was a sign reading 'toilets' and an arrow pointing down a narrow passage beyond the telephone. This sounded like a refuge. I put a handkerchief to my mouth and edged past Ferguson.

'I don't see what the hell good my name'll do you!' he snapped as I passed, and slammed the phone down. Then he turned and looked me full in the face, or at least in what he could see of my face.

Probably the handkerchief helped him to identify me. A bearded man he might have ignored. But I must have looked like an acquaintance having a sneeze.

'Jesus Christ!' he said. 'If it isn't the woman-terrorizer himself!'

He gripped me violently by the arm, obviously quite ready to do battle, and seemed surprised when I stood quite still. I didn't want to draw attention to myself, not now. Not with the police outside.

'Let's find the police,' he said viciously, as if reading my thought.

'You weren't so keen just now,' I replied with an attempt at a debonair smile.

'What the hell do you mean?'

'I've no time to talk now,' I said. 'Let's find the police. Let's tell them about Moira Jane. *All* about Moira Jane. Let's tell everyone. Annic. Your wife.'

I could see he believed me at once.

He went white. I thought he was going to hit me. I wouldn't have blamed him. I didn't much like what I was doing either. But I went on.

'I've seen the photographs as well,' I lied urgently. 'I reckon with a bit of ingenuity, I could get hold of copies.'

He was still uncertain, on a knife's edge, not knowing what to do. I had to make up his mind for him.

'We can't just stand here,' I said. 'If I'm caught now, I talk. Let's get to your car.'

115

Without a word he led the way out. I climbed into the passenger seat, ignoring the policeman who was still hanging around. But I didn't stop sweating till we were a mile along the road. Then I started shaking.

He drove like a maniac along those narrow, twisty roads. Neither of us spoke. I didn't want to risk losing the small ascendancy I had. He, I knew, would be busily debating in his mind what was best to do.

'Did you hurt her?' he asked finally, his voice level and controlled.

'Who?'

'Moira Jane.'

'No,' I said. 'She's been looking after me. She called the police because I left. That's all.'

'Why were you calling?' I asked. 'She wasn't expecting you. And I thought you didn't come unless summoned.'

He didn't reply but the furrows on his brow deepened in anger.

'You weren't just checking up, were you?' I said. 'Just to see if she was there? Of course, she should have left by now, shouldn't she? That's it.' I was suddenly certain. 'You were going to have a look, weren't you? See what you could find! It must have been a shock when a man answered!'

I laughed, softly.

'Bentink,' he said. The car was doing sixty-five. 'Bentink, did you kill those girls?'

I knew he wanted to be convinced of my innocence. It would make things easier for him. I'd no desire to help the bastard, but I had to help myself.

I told him the full story as far as I could. Details were already growing surprisingly dim in my mind. As I finished, he turned into the driveway of a large house and halted. We were somewhere on the outskirts of Cockermouth.

'Where's this?' I said.

'It's where I'm staying,' he replied. 'Don't worry. Our friends are out.'

A long silence. Then he turned to me, and smiled. I didn't

116

trust his smile. But I knew he'd made the only decision he could make.

'Right, Bentink. You win. Not because of your threats, mind you, but because it seems likely to me you're innocent.'

It's always easy to reach a conclusion you want to reach, I thought, but kept the thought to myself.

'What are your plans?' he asked.

'I don't know.'

He explored his beard with a thumb and made me scratch my own sympathetically. Suddenly he snapped his forefinger out and pointed it at me, a powerful gesture.

'Look,' he said with the blunt sincerity which must have gone down big on the television. 'Why don't you give yourself up? I'll do all I can. That man Melton struck me as being a very reasonable kind of fellow. It's the sensible thing to do.'

From his point of view, it was the sensible thing to do. It would get me nicely off his hands. It didn't matter whether he believed me or not. Here he was, stuck with and longing to be rid of me. Natural envy has always made me reluctant to be impressed by the famous, but Ferguson seemed to be bent on making the process more than commonly difficult.

'No,' I said, 'I don't think so. I'll be on my way in a minute.'

I imagined his face brightened beneath its hair.

'But before I go, fill me in on what's happened. It's a week now since I got away and I haven't heard or seen a news report since.'

'Well,' he began, 'you'll be able to make a fortune I should think if you are . . . if you can prove yourself innocent. Some of the papers have really gone to town. Nothing direct, you know, but it doesn't take more than a chat at the local and a salacious mind to put two and two together. I reckon the cumulative effect is libellous. They've dug up everything about Thorne, of course. Just the facts, his job at the University, his time in hospital. Just the facts; at least, I assume they are facts insomuch as they dare print them. He comes out of it all as a pretty disturbed character.'

'He is a pretty disturbed character,' I replied. 'Is that all?'

'Not all,' he said. 'They've got you painted in pretty odd colours too. And your Lakeland journeys are beginning to sound like the advance of the Germans into France.'

'What about my wife?'

'There's no sign of her. No one knows where she went. Another week and I reckon they'll be hinting you left her in a box at some left-luggage office. You've been sighted everywhere. You even scared a couple of nurses in the gardens of Worcester Infirmary only last night.'

He chuckled. I didn't. I was cursing the ill-fortune which had localized the search once again.

'Where is Peter?' I asked.

'He's in the hospital wing of Durham gaol. There's not much news about him. Just reports on his past.'

'Are there any signs that the police are still working at the case?' I asked desperately. 'They can't have just given up and settled for us.'

'Why not? You're very good runners, both of you. You must have felt pretty certain that Melton had you cornered or you wouldn't have made a run for it.'

'Cornered?' I said with a laugh. 'He was reading the charge out.'

He looked at me keenly.

'But you told me there were just the two of you?'

'That's right.'

Ferguson barked a laugh.

'Then it was just a try-on. He wouldn't charge you alone. I doubt if it's legal. He must have been pushing you to see how far you'd go.'

I shrugged my shoulders with indifference. Even if it had been just a 'try-on,' it had had the same result as if I'd been guilty.

I looked at Ferguson and wondered if I could squeeze a few more miles out of him then decided it wasn't worth it.

'I'd better be off then,' I said, and opened the car door.

'Right,' he said.

I got out.

'Bentink,' he said. 'Look. Take these.'

He handed me from the back of the car a light coat and a Robin Hood hat. I took them with surprise and thanked him, thinking even as I did so that he probably reckoned they'd help me to get a bit further away from him before I was recaptured.

'It'll cover up that horrid brown suit anyway,' he said, pointing to the coat.

I put it on, and the hat, thinking that apart from my shoes, I was not wearing a single thing that belonged to me.

'Good luck,' he said.

'Thanks,' I said, and turned to go. I had only taken a couple of steps down the drive when I realized I was going to need all the good luck I could get. Coming towards me was Annie Ferguson.

I must have caused a real confusion in her mind. She stared at me in great puzzlement. She obviously half-recognized the hat and coat and half-recognized the bearded figure wearing them, but could not quite put the two together.

She stopped about two yards from me.

'Hello, Annie,' I said.

Recognition erupted in her eyes and she took a couple of steps to the car.

'Father,' she began anxiously.

Ferguson, who had seen her in the mirror, began to get out.

'It's all right, Annie,' he said.

She clung on to his arm.

'Has he hurt you?'

'No, dear.'

'I'll ring the police.'

'Wait!'

She stopped in obedience to her father's command.

'What's going on, Father?'

'I believe Mr Bentink is innocent, my dear.'

She peered closely into his face, looking, I felt, for any signs of coercement. Then, apparently satisfied, with a frightening display of faith she turned to me.

'I'm sorry, Mr Bentink,' she said in very formal tones.

'For what?'

'For whatever you have had cause to resent in my behaviour.'

I rubbed the back of my head and smiled.

'I'm glad you've finally reasoned your way to the truth,' I said.

She flushed a little but stood her ground.

'I find you a difficult man to trust, Mr Bentink, but my father I trust implicitly.'

He put his arm round her shoulder. I raised my hands as though holding a camera and said, 'Smile please.'

They didn't.

'Well, goodbye then.'

I turned once more but was stopped almost immediately by Annie's voice, which was filled with surprising anxiety.

'Wait! Where are you going?'

'Just taking a stroll down the road, ma'am,' I said.

'You can't do that. I saw two policemen within a couple of minutes as I walked here. You'd be picked up in no time.'

She turned to her father for support and advice and I grinned ironically at Ferguson. He had the power by a word to persuade his daughter of my innocence. Could he equally rapidly persuade her that it was best to let an innocent man stroll into the hands of the police who wished to charge him with murder?

He didn't even try. He values his daughter's picture of him greatly, I thought. A good job for me he does. Some old fast-fading self-image momentarily raised its eyebrows at my easy acceptance of blackmail. But the new self-image shrugged and listened in amusement to Ferguson.

'No, you're right, dear. You mustn't go yet, Bentink. Are Mary and Joe home yet, Annie?'

'I'll see,' she said, and set off towards the house. Mary and Joe, I deduced, were the friends they were staying with.

'Nice girl, Annie,' I said.

'Don't push your luck, Bentink,' he said in the broadest Scots accent I had heard him use.

Annie came back very quickly.

'No, the car's not in the garage.'

'Right,' said Ferguson, climbing back into his car. 'Let's move.'

Five minutes later, I was sitting in a very comfortable armchair drinking a large glass of Scotch. I had been briefed to head out of the kitchen door and down to a small garden shed the second Mary and Joe's car was heard approaching. I hoped they would take their time. I was very comfortable.

Ferguson and Annie were both more concerned about the immediate future than I could make myself be. But the only connection between their worryings was that I was their object. Any resemblance ended there. Ferguson wanted rid of me for his own sake. Annie wanted rid of me for mine (and she imagined her father felt this way too). She therefore was concerned with my next destination while her father would gladly have dropped me naked on the heights of Skiddaw.

I smiled at his dilemma and added fuel to the fire of his distraction by saying to Annie,

'All right. Get me to Carlisle.'

This definite aim was as great a satisfaction to her as it was an additional trouble to her father.

'It's impossible,' he said. 'The place must be crawling with policemen. They'll be stopping everything.'

I felt this was a bit of an exaggeration but was saved from saying so by Annie who said it for me.

'There are too many back roads,' she said. 'With side-lights, after dark, you'll never be noticed.'

121

Ferguson looked as if he would argue further, but a car was heard coming up the drive. I leapt up.

'All right then,' he said. 'Lie low till I come for you. We'll do our best.'

With what was rapidly becoming a well-practised agility, I ran lightly through the kitchen and down the garden to the shed. There, seated in a dark corner on an upturned bucket with garden implements and smells all around, I analyzed this decision of Ferguson's with the cynicism which seemed to be affecting all my thoughts about this man and decided that I would be asked to get out of the car after a token couple of miles. I couldn't really blame him, I thought. After all, I was nothing to him except a potential source of trouble. My real nuisance value, of course, was that I had somehow become a symbol to Annie of her father's love of justice, freedom and a lot of other abstractions. It was better than being a villain anyway, I reflected, and settled down to wait for the darkness to close in around the shed.

ELEVEN

If nothing else good had come out of my activities of the last seven days, at least I had learnt to enjoy sitting doing nothing, in no matter what discomfort. When the door finally creaked open three or more hours later, I was disappointed rather than pleased. A beam of light sprang from a torch (*that* torch again, I thought) and moved around till it found me. I smiled inanely like a comedian staring into a darkened auditorium.

'Time to go,' whispered a voice.

I screwed my eyes up and peered behind the torch. It wasn't Ferguson, it was Annie.

'Where's your father?'

'He's stuck inside with an old bird-watcher friend who just turned up. He can't get away, so I invented a visit and slipped out.'

That'd please Ferguson no end, I thought.

'Get a move on,' she said.

I got a move on. It was a bright clear night with only the faintest of breezes. Further down the garden in a clump of rhododendrons a bird burst into song for a moment, then was silent.

She pointed me down the drive and went to get the car. A minute later I was sitting beside her as we turned out of the gates on to the road.

'Here we go again,' I said.

She didn't reply and I sat in silence beside her watching the hedgerows gliding by. We had decided I might as well sit in the front too. If we were stopped I had as much chance of bluffing it out as of remaining concealed. I still wore Ferguson's hat and coat.

After a short distance we turned on to a minor road and then on to one more minor still till eventually we were speeding along lanes no wider it seemed than the car. She was driving on sidelights only, and clear though the night was, I felt my hands sweating every time we swung round a corner.

Once as we approached a junction with a slightly wider road, she stopped the car and turned off lights and engine. A few moments later the crossroads was filled with light as another car swept across our path. She let it fade out of sight and hearing before starting up again. I had not even been aware of its approach and yet every one of my senses seemed to be super-alert.

We moved so swiftly and silently that several times we narrowly missed small animals scuttling over the road and once we both ducked instinctively as an owl swept in front of us, almost brushing the windscreen with his wing.

We came up a slight rise and pulled to a halt once more.

When I looked at her questioningly, she pointed ahead. In the distance was a line of lights which could only be a main road. Faintly we could see the headlights of cars as they twisted their way along. At roughly the same spot they all seemed to hesitate, slow down, stop. Then they started up again. We watched this happen half a dozen times.

'They're stopping cars,' she said. 'They've picked a good spot too.'

She put the car into reverse and used a gateway to turn round. The dreamlike ride began again, but after a while it became less smooth than before and she seemed to be peering out into the darkness with less confidence. Finally we stopped again at another junction.

'I'm a bit lost,' she said. 'It was having to change our route back there. But that looks like a signpost.'

She seized our mutual friend, the torch, and we got out together and peered up at the worn flaked letters.

'Thurbeck,' she read. 'That doesn't help.'

124

It didn't help her, but it helped me. At least it might. I stood and weighed matters in my mind.

She was back in the car and I felt her impatience. I got in beside her.

'You've been thinking a lot,' she said with some irritation. 'You decide which way we go.'

'Go to Thurbeck,' I said.

Without another word, she started up and we coasted phantom-like down a long undulating and winding road till the lights of a tiny hamlet came into view. She slowed down, uncertain. I put my hand out to hers on the steering wheel.

'Turn off the road, on the right, just ahead. There. Now pull her round behind the hedge.'

We came to a halt in an uncultivated field which slanted awkwardly across the diagonal from the corner we now occupied. In the bottommost corner was the dim bulk of a cottage with a thin line of light down the middle of a thickly-curtained window the only sign of habitation.

'Why have we stopped here?' Annie asked in a steady, clear voice.

My hand was still on hers. I took it away and pointed to the cottage.

'My father-in-law lives there.'

I had not spared old Will a thought in months. It had taken the signpost to remind me how close I was to him. Whether he would help or not, I didn't know. But I felt certain he would not hinder and that his mouth would remain shut.

'Won't the police know and be watching?' asked Annie.

This was a good point. I thought for a moment.

'No. Not if they haven't interviewed my wife yet. Your father said he thought they hadn't found her, that she was abroad. Is this what you've read?'

'Yes,' she said. We sat in silence a while longer. I was strangely reluctant to leave the car.

'Tell me, Mr Bentink,' she said, 'as a matter of interest,

not of doubt, how did you persuade my father of your innocence?'

'It was easy,' I said. 'He spoke to a passing angel and got the full story.'

She let out a little hiss of anger. It was easier to leave the car now.

'I'm going down there,' I said. 'Thanks a lot for the ride. I am truly grateful.'

'Don't be a fool,' said Annie. 'You can't just go barging in. You never know who's there. Why take the risk? We can still get to Carlisle.'

'That's pretty dangerous, and for you too. This way there'll just be one of us at risk.'

How altruistic can you get, I thought. She got out of the car on the other side and came round to me.

'I'll come down with you then. If it's no go, you can come back to the car. If it's all right, I'll just fade away and go home.'

'Look,' I said, 'what's your interest? Why are you doing this?'

'You're innocent,' she said with a touching simplicity. 'I coshed you once. I owe you for that. And it must be a terrible thing to be falsely accused of such a crime. You need help.'

I could find nothing to say to that but my hesitation was not prolonged as suddenly the headlights of a car blazed over the rise of the road then levelled down towards us.

'Duck!' I said and caught her in my arms and crouched down behind the hedge.

The car drove on by down the hill without slowing. I let out my held breath.

Annie was pressed tightly to me and I released my grip, but she just pressed herself tighter, her face buried in my shoulder. I pulled her hair gently and her head moved back, then her mouth came up to mine and she kissed me with a violence of passion that took me by surprise. But my Superboy body soon recovered and I applied myself to the activity with great enthusiasm. After a short while her

126

tongue in my mouth and my hands in her car-coat were not enough and I rocked forward to a kneeling position and laid her on the ground before me. She breathed something inaudible, never opened her eyes, but her hands came up and caressed my face and beard.

Desire failed in me as I felt those eager fingers burying themselves in the shallow tangles of my beard and looked down at that passion-flushed face and close-shut eyes. I knelt there quite still and looked down at her. After a while the hands stopped moving and the eyes opened. She looked up at me without expression, then the hands fell away. She sat up and looked at her slender legs, forking out from flimsy white briefs. She pulled her skirt down and stood up.

I got up beside her and we set off down the diagonal slope to the cottage. My legs were weak beneath me and I stumbled against her twice. She accepted my weight without any attempt at evasion.

We covered the last few yards to the cottage with great stealth, partly for fear of disturbing the inmates, and partly because, though fairly isolated, the cottage was on the fringe of the hamlet and there were another couple of houses quite close on the same lane. We, of course, coming across the field, were approaching the back door.

We crouched down and pressed ourselves close to the wall by the window.

The crack of light where the curtains did not quite meet was so thin that I could see little or nothing at first. It was not till I had moved my eyes up and down the whole length of it that I found a spot where the width was sufficient to allow me to see in. Even then I could only see a very narrow sliver of the room. Across it moved old Will. He was talking, but I couldn't hear what he said, nor see who he was talking to. I hoped it was only his wife. But I had to be certain.

I sank back down, wondering whether I should get Annie to knock at the door under some pretext. But what? She would have to get right in for it to be any use. Then my doubts were put at rest by a sound made familiar by Jan's accounts of her childhood, reluctantly told in our early days together when we were still fascinatedly exploring each other's minds and bodies – the thrusting home of the great metal bolts (three of them) on the back door, a process shortly to be repeated at the front.

The point was that the nightly locking-up ritual would not take place with visitors in the house. Visitors, I gathered, were such a rarity in any case that I need hardly have feared them.

I walked boldly to the back door and banged hard against it.

Nothing happened. Then 'Who's there?' quavered the voice of Mary, Jan's mother, followed immediately by Will's deeper 'Hist, woman,' and the sound of bolts being withdrawn. The ancient door creaked open and Will stood there, framed in the darkness.

'Come in, lad,' he said in the same tone he would have used had I come in broad daylight and expected. Then he saw Annie. 'Wha's this?'

'A friend. She helped me.'

'Come along in, miss.'

We crowded into the darkened kitchen. Mary stood looking at us without a word.

'Let's go through,' said Will.

He pushed open the living-room door and the rectangle of light fell into the kitchen. I stepped aside and motioned Annie through first. She moved forward, then came to a dead halt in the doorway. I pressed close against her and had time to register the sensuous pressure of the curve of her buttocks before I saw what had caused her to halt.

Standing facing us, her face mobile with uncertainty, was Jan.

I was tired of surprises. I was tired of making sudden readjustments to circumstances and people. I felt a sudden flood of nostalgia not for my old life but for the peace and the darkness of the garden shed I had sat in waiting for Ferguson.

The sight of Jan filled me illogically with resentment. Something of this must have shown for the uncertainty went out of her face and she said in a perfectly self-possessed tone: 'Hello, Harry.'

I pushed by Annie and confronted my wife.

'What are you doing here?' I asked ungraciously. She did not reply but looked at Annie.

'Who's this?'

There was the thinnest edge of a sneer in her tone and Annie reacted to it. Ignoring Jan she turned to me and, in perfect imitation, echoed, 'Who's this?'

'My wife,' I answered, then turned it into an introduction. 'This is Annie Ferguson. She helped me get here.'

'That *was* kind of you, dear,' said Jan.

The stresses and intonation were perfect and Annie went stiff. Then Will, whom we had all forgotten, let out a chuckle behind us.

'Hear that, Mary? Our Jan could always take off people to a turn, eh?'

This reduction of Jan's performance to the status of a performance eased the tension for a moment, cooling Annie's anger and melting the icy façade which Jan had built around herself. I took a step towards her.

'I'm glad to see you, Jan,' I said.

She looked at me searchingly.

'Let's all sit down,' said Will. 'You'll be ready for a drink.'

'So will you,' I said, and he smiled broadly.

'Ay, you bugger,' he said, 'I'm always ready.'

He poured four great tumblerfuls of whisky. His wife did not drink. She sat still and alert in a corner while the rest of us were grouped around the great open fireplace. There was no fire at this time of year, but a splendid arrangement of green and red ferns in a bowl lit up the grate.

'Who'll start?' I asked after taking a long pull at my glass.

'I think you had best,' said Will. 'Did you kill those lasses?'

I looked at him as he sat in the perfect ease of a man in

charge of his own house. He wore a collarless shirt with its sleeves cut off a couple of inches above the elbow, and a much-darned and much-holed short-sleeved pullover; his ancient trousers dated back to a period when he measured a great deal less in girth and they were unbuttoned at the top to ease his waist. On his feet were a pair of ex-army boots, with their laces undone and trailing as a concession to domestic use.

His question to me sounded like (and I felt sure was) merely a request for a necessary piece of information. No condition of assistance was being put forward here.

'No,' I said.

'Can you prove it?' put in Jan.

'Of course he can't,' said Will, 'or he wouldn't be here.'

'I think she means, can I prove it to you, Will,' I said.

He nodded.

'You're the only one here who can *prove* it to me, Jan. Could he do it?'

I looked across at her but she evaded my gaze.

'I don't know,' she said. 'I don't know. How *can* I know?'

She looked around for assistance. I sympathized with her predicament. How could anyone *know* anyone else perfectly. The best we could offer was blind faith. But Mary in the corner on whom Jan's eyes had finally settled, spoke.

'I know what your father could do and could not do, lass. Do you think I'd spend my life with a man if I did not know what he was?'

This was probably the most complex speech I had ever heard her utter. Even Will looked up with a slight smile on his lips. Jan nodded a couple of times, in thought rather than acquiescence it seemed to me, then she turned to look at me once more. Perhaps it was just my fancy that made me sense she was letting into her mind with long missed clarity all the course of our life together, probing into all the corners where violence might lie hidden and certainly looking at every aspect of our physical relationship. The enthusiasm, the abandon, the readiness, the odd times and

130

strange places, the seductions – and the mock-rapes. But running through it all, if our love had not been one-sided, she must have sensed and remembered the sweetness of it, the recognition of who we were, the refusal ever to become each other's thing.

'No,' she said finally. 'He could not do it. He can do much that is cruel, but not that.'

This qualification of her verdict cut short any immodest satisfaction I might have felt and I nearly turned on her with the kind of self-controlled sarcasm which was the harbinger of so many of our quarrels. But an awareness of where we were and what we were doing caught me before I spoke. Incredibly I felt glad that I was here with all the attendant circumstances rather than alone with Jan about to file another layer off our marriage.

'Why are you here, Jan?' I asked. 'I mean, not that I don't want you here, don't misunderstand me.'

Will shook his head slightly at the thought of a man's wife having the temerity to misunderstand him, but Jan nodded her comprehension.

'You mean, am I here because of this business. No, not really. Though I might have come when it happened. I came up a week ago. I didn't know what to do with myself when you and Peter went on holiday. I had no one I wanted to go with.'

She busied herself with her drink for a moment, while the casually spoken confession sank into my consciousness. Then she resumed.

'So on an impulse I came up here. It happened on the day I arrived. I didn't know about it till I got here and Mam told me. They'd heard it on the radio and thought it was just a coincidence of names that the escaped man was called Bentink. But I knew.'

'Why didn't you come forward?' I asked.

Will answered. 'We knew you'd either be caught or come here. It was daft our Jan letting herself be questioned by a lot of policemen when she couldn't even see you. So I made her put her car in the old barn up hill. She'd arrived too late for folks around here to be up to see her. And she's stuck close to the house ever since.'

'And you told no one you were coming?' I said, fearful that the house might be watched.

'Who should I tell?' she replied.

I thought of her circle of women friends, the ones who would have been so eager to pass on to the police the rumour of our breaking marriage, and shrugged my shoulders.

Annie, I noticed, was sitting perfectly still except for her eyes which flicked from speaker to speaker, missing nothing. There was a possible problem here, but whose it was, hers or mine, I had not yet decided. In any case this was not the time and place for problems of any kind except the great problem of my next move. I mentally shifted both Jan and Annie out of the arena of thought and made myself concentrate on the situation before me. Jan settled back in her chair with something like resignation on her face. Annie helped herself to another Scotch despite a disapproving look from Will, who believed that to offer one drink to a woman was generous, but a second was merely frivolous.

'Right,' I said, 'I take it all assembled are for whatever reasons believers in my innocence? Good. Then let's look at the problem which seems to me to be twofold.'

I was beginning to get into my board-meeting stride and was a little put out when Will reached forward and tapped me on the knee.

'Tell us your story first, lad.'

I baulked a bit at this, partly I suppose because I'd already been through the thing once today with Ferguson, partly because, as I said to them, there was nothing I could say to them which I hadn't said to Melton.

'But he was looking for proof of your guilt, not of your innocence.'

This was from Jan. I looked from her to her father and thought with surprise how alike they looked, not so much

132

in feature as in the relaxed attentiveness of their postures. Suddenly, absurdly, I felt the stirring of a hope that this ill-assorted pair might really be able to help me.

'All right, if you must,' I said, and began my account of all that happened from our arrival at the Derwent Hotel till the police picked us up at Ravenglass. Here I paused.

'Go on,' said Will, so I related the course of my interrogation by Melton and all that had come out of it. When I reached the bit about Peter and Marco, I watched Jan covertly, but no other expression showed on her face than the calm attentiveness she had displayed throughout.

'You're up against it, lad,' said Will when I finished. 'A man on bad terms with his woman and a queer out of a loony-bin, that's a bad enough start. Then there's the barman who saw you trying to get off with the lasses and there's half a dozen others who are ready to say you were a bad lot. You sound like a couple of drunks, that's bad too.' He shook his head and took a long pull at his glass.

'But that's not the worst. There's the fact that you met these lasses, that you lied about it and that you didn't admit your lie till witnesses were produced. Then there's the blood from the sheep. And the funny way you behaved later, and the things your friend said to this lass's father' – indicating Annie – 'And if that wasn't enough, there's the fact that your friend has confessed, or so they say. That's a strong case.'

'You're forgetting one thing,' said Jan quietly.

'Aye, and what's that?'

'The fact that Harry ran away. He could have had the best legal and other expert advice during the past week. He could perhaps have caused some kind of doubt in this man, Melton's, mind. He doesn't sound a fool. But the trail's cold too. And probably all Melton's been doing for the past seven days is directing the search after you, Harry.'

It was only the matter-of-fact tone of voice with no hint of reproach in it that prevented me from answering very sharply.

She went on. 'The only positive thing I can see so far is

133

that they can't make me give evidence that our marriage was breaking up. But that's not much.'

'Go through it again, Harry,' said Will.

I did so and this time he laboriously noted down in his round board-school hand times and places. He sat then and looked for some minutes at the piece of wrapping paper on which he had made his annotations.

Finally I said, 'Well?'

He looked up. 'Don't be in such a bloody hurry, lad. If it was easy, don't you think that some little bobby would have done it? Any road, there's no need to bother your head about where to go next. You'll stay here tonight and as long as you need.'

'No.'

It was Mary. We had forgotten about her again, perched like a little bird in her corner.

'No,' she repeated when we all turned and looked at her.

'What do you mean, "no"?' asked Will more in puzzlement than in anger.

She stood up.

'You can stay tonight and welcome,' she said to me. 'You're Jan's husband, and I like you yourself as far as that goes. But I'll not let Will be caught as an accessory.'

She had some difficulty with the word, but got it out correct in the end.

'What are you saying, woman?' roared Will.

But his wife was unimpressed.

'I've asked. I thought this might happen, so I asked. Not openly, but just in passing. They say you can get five years as an accessory. It's not worth five years of Will's life.'

Will bellowed at her so loudly that I had to make him be quiet before the neighbours, distant though they were, heard him. But Mary was adamant.

'You'll have more sense than him, Harry. You understand these things.'

134

'He stays in my house as long as I want, woman!' roared Will.

Mary took the clock off the mantelpiece, her inevitable preliminary to going to bed. At the door she turned and looked her husband in the face.

'If he doesn't go tomorrow, I'll tell the constable he's here. Then we wouldn't be accessories. Goodnight, Jan, goodnight, Harry, goodnight, miss.'

With this she left us to listen to Will's rantings which went on some time before they died down.

'It's not you, Harry,' he said, 'it's me. The silly woman's thinking of me.'

'I know,' I said. 'And she's right. In any case, I couldn't have stopped here long. They're bound to get a line on you sooner or later. It's a wonder someone in the village hasn't spoken up already.'

'Oh, they're close folk round here,' said Will. 'But you could be right. Still, you're all right tonight.'

'Harry,' said Annie, 'I'd better go. It's very late and Father will be worried. Can I help you tomorrow?'

I stood up with her.

'No,' I said, 'you've done enough already. I'm very grateful.'

She turned to Will and Jan.

'Goodbye,' she said. 'I know everything will turn out all right.'

'Goodbye, lass,' said Will. Jan merely nodded.

I went with Annie into the kitchen and opened the door for her. It was very dark outside.

'I'll come with you to the car,' I said, but she put her hand on my chest and restrained.

'No, it's silly taking the risk when you're here. I'll be all right.'

I reached up and took her hand.

'Thanks again.'

She looked at me then brought her other hand up to my face.

135

'Get a shave,' she said, pulled away and was gone.

'What did that mean?' said Jan from the open door behind me.

'Nothing, I don't know,' which was just about the truth. I passed back into the living-room where Will was studying his piece of paper again. He looked up.

'It's late for talk. You two will be ready for bed, I reckon.'

I could not tell from his face how deliberately ambiguous his remark was but in the surface sense at least he was right. Even three hours' relaxation in a potting shed is no substitute for sleep in a bed. I looked at Jan a bit uncertainly, however. There were only two bedrooms in the place as I recalled, Will and Mary's and a narrow boxroom of a place. Jan and I had not slept together since the night I told her of my plan to go on holiday with Peter. That had been a fortnight before the holiday started, but we had been nowhere nearer a reconciliation before I left.

She said, 'You go on up. I'll be up in a minute.'

I went carefully up the narrow creaking stairs and let myself into the bedroom which, though I had only seen it once on a brief tour of the cottage (we'd never actually stayed there, of course), was exactly as I had pictured it. Very small, with a single bed pushed against the wall.

At least this aspect of our feud would end here, I thought with half a smile. In these conditions, togetherness was a must.

How far the togetherness might have gone I never found out. Jan came in when I was half undressed. She stood and stared at me, then said, 'Harry, you never said where you'd been for the past five days. What *were* you doing?'

There was a keener note than curiosity in her voice and the reason was not far to seek. I realized that I was standing there wearing a pair of yellow knickers and round my feet were the remnants of three pairs of nylons. I didn't even attempt to explain, not then, not there. I felt I looked ludicrous. I also felt so tired I didn't give a damn.

'Not now, Jan,' I said. 'Not now. Come to bed.'

136

I pulled back the coverlet and started to clamber in.

'I'll sit up for a while with my father,' she said, and turned and left.

I stood with one foot still on the floor then shrugged and burrowed down beneath the sheets. The pillow smelt of Jan's hair lacquer and my last waking thought was to wonder why she used hair lacquer in a place like this.

I was awoken by a pressure on my shoulder. I grunted, thinking that Jan had at last come to bed and was not being very considerate about waking me, and pressed up against the wall. But the pressure only increased and became a shaking. I turned round and peered blearily up.

It was indeed Jan, but she was fully dressed.

'Come on,' she said. 'Time to go.'

I stopped myself from saying 'Go where?' or something equally pointless, and climbed sleepily out of bed. It was just first light so I couldn't have had more than four hours' sleep. A cock crew in the distance.

'Sound effects, too,' I muttered, scratching my itchy face noisily.

'Take your girl-friend's advice and get that off. And here. Put these on.'

She flung a pair of almost knee-length underpants, obviously Will's, on the bed. I picked them up and looked at them incredulously.

'Suit yourself,' she said. 'If they catch you in those things' (pointing to the yellow pants I was still wearing), 'they'll lock you up without a trial.'

It seemed a case of Hobson's choice to me, but I stood up and removed the knickers and pulled on the semi-long Johns. Jan stirred the yellow pants with her toe; spreading them out so that their full size was apparent.

'You're right,' I said, feeling the viciousness of early-rising, 'they're too big to be Annie's.'

'So I see. Then they must belong to that woman in Ennerdale.'

She had also brought me a shirt of Will's as a substitute

for Moira Jane's pullover, and I stopped with this half over my head then slowly pulled it down as she went on.

'That's where you stayed the last five days, isn't it?'

I had wondered why no one had mentioned the news report of my 'rape' of Moira Jane the previous night and had decided that for some reason they could not have had their radio on that day. To mention it myself had seemed a needless complication.

'How do you work that out?' I asked.

'Well, we presumed your innocence on the same grounds as before, that is, my wifely instinct.'

She showed her protruding teeth in a faint smile – or sneer – and began spraying her hair with an aerosol hair-lacquer tube. I coughed as the thin haze drifted my way. She knew I hated the stuff.

'Therefore,' she went on, 'as you were obviously in such good health when you got here, and as obviously you had only recently came under the aegis of Miss Ferguson – whose volte-face from bashing you on the head was never fully explained – it seemed likely that someone else had been looking after you indoors. You must have some connection with this woman – apart from the one *she* alleges of course – or you wouldn't be wearing her husband's suit.'

She picked up the jacket I had hung on the door knob and showed me the name tag stitched in the collar.

'Therefore, it seems likely you stayed with her, she gave you food, shelter, comfort, and her knickers. But when you left, for some reason she decided to turn you in. Right?'

It was quite remarkably right, of course. But all I did was to applaud ironically and say, 'And have the famous loving father/daughter team had any success with their *major* investigation of the moment? Can we expect an early answer?'

She did not like what I said, and I instantly regretted it. Just how permanent this rapprochement with her father was I had still to find out, but now was not the time.

But she answered my question as though it had been straightforward.

'No. I'm sorry. Nothing yet. There are too many intangibles. We'd need to see everybody's statements and all we've got is what you can tell us and what has been printed in the papers. Someone must be lying, but it's probably someone we've never even heard of. And the trouble is that you yourself cannot deny the things which make up the bulk of the police case.'

'Tell me something I don't know,' I growled, and went downstairs to the kitchen to have a wash. The house had no bathroom, only a large tin tub for use in front of the living-room fire. I could imagine the agonies which Jan must have suffered in her early teens.

Will was downstairs, obviously having sat up all night. He was surrounded by newspapers and had bits of paper marked with his own round scribble all over the table.

I asked if he had a razor I could borrow and received with some trepidation a formidable-looking cut-throat. It almost lived up to its name several times, but finally I was satisfied I had removed my whiskers but left a narrow military moustache which, with the aid of Ferguson's hat and coat, I felt would make me difficult to recognize from either of my two current descriptions. I smiled at the thought that with the general public now looking for me with beard whilst still used to the picture of me clean-shaven, twice the normally large number of 'sightings' would probably be reported.

Jan came into the kitchen while I was shaving and made some coffee and toast.

'What's the master-plan?' I asked jocularly. She turned on me with a ferocity which took me by surprise.

'Listen, Harry, we're sticking our necks out for you, so drop the superiority act.'

This was Jan getting back to her best bitchiness form. I replied in kind.

'I didn't ask you to help me. I didn't even know you were here. And I've managed pretty well on my own so far.'

'You mean your women have managed pretty well for you. And you came here of your own choice to try to get my father's help, didn't you? You're really lost without all the little men in the office to run around after you, so you just latch on to the nearest possible support. Face up to yourself, Harry.'

I surprised myself by roaring with genuine laughter, not the artificial sort I sometimes used when Jan got under my guard. I suppose inherited power is always a subject for self-doubt and guilt-feelings, but the little bit of commercial power I had been left by my father had just recently come to appear a rather infantile game.

'Pow!' I said to Jan, waving the razor threateningly. 'You have obviously not yet met Superboy. Wham! Kerzoink!'

She backed away as I approached, but the kitchen table stopped her retreat. She was obviously uncertain what to make of my outburst and I laughed again, then put my arms around her and kissed her with an exaggerated passion. But the feel of those protruding teeth pressing into my lip and the grip of her hand tightening round my shoulders soon had me overtaking my exaggeration.

'The toast's burning,' said Will. 'And folk get up early round here, so you'd better save that. You should try getting a wife who goes to bed at night.'

I disengaged myself reluctantly.

'It's such a *big* table too,' I whispered to Jan, whose eyes were shining as I had not seen them shine for a long time. She giggled and rescued the toast and we had a quick breakfast in the living-room, while she told me the 'master-plan.'

It was quite simple, really. She had gone out earlier and got her car out of the old barn. It was now parked a quarter of a mile along the road, hidden in a field entrance and, unlike the barn, quite out of sight of any habitation. We were to cut along the fields at the back of the cottage and reach the road (which was the continuation of the one Annie and I had been on the previous night, but on the other side of the

140

village) without going near the houses. Then we were going to make our way across to the A6, the main north-south trunk road and head down to London.

'Or anywhere else we decide. The thing is to get a start,' said Jan.

'Well, Will, it's been no use then?' I said to the old man, who was still studying his bits of paper.

'Aye,' he said. 'I hoped I could get at something just by a comparison of what you said with what the papers say these others said. But there isn't much. Can't print it, I daresay. You have a look.'

I took the bits of paper, but Jan rose and said, 'Come on. We'd better get moving before they start milking the cows over at the big farm.'

She'd taken her own case with her in the night so we'd nothing to encumber us.

'Goodbye, Will,' I said. 'Thanks for your help.'

'It was nought,' he said. 'I hoped I could do more.'

Strangely, I now realized, so had I despite my scoffing. I shook his hand with real gratitude, however, and turned to find Mary in the doorway. Jan kissed her.

'Goodbye, Mam,' she said.

'Goodbye, love,' said Mary, then, taking my hand, she said, 'Don't think I mean you harm, Harry.'

'I know you don't. Goodbye, Mary.'

I kissed her cheek. She squeezed my hand.

'There may be good come of all this yet,' she said.

'Goodbye, Dad,' said Jan. I looked at her in surprise. This was the first time I had heard her call her father (always referred to indirectly as 'my father') anything at all to his face. She pulled my sleeve.

'Come on, hurry up,' she said, and after the back door had been unbarred, unbolted and unlocked, we set out into the early morning.

There was a light mist rising from the field and we were soon out of sight of the cottage and the village. Our real isolation was increased tenfold by this flimsy haze which hung about us like breathing in a frosty air. Our initial stealth soon disappeared and we walked side by side, our arms round each other, not speaking. It was almost too early for the birds but a few were singing, merry and clear.

'How far?' I asked.

'Nearly there,' she said.

The grass beneath our feet was beaded with dew and we shook a little spray into the air with each step.

'Over there,' she said, and ahead through the mist I saw the black line of the hedge which marked the road. As we approached we had to pass through a small clump of four or five beech trees. Their leafy branches linked overhead and the ground here was mossy and untouched by dew. I paused and looked at Jan.

'Yes?' I said interrogatively.

'Oh yes,' she said.

It was half an hour later and the mist had risen when we reached the car.

TWELVE

Neither of us spoke as we drove along the empty lanes. I had offered to drive, thinking Jan might need the sleep after her wakeful night, but she had refused. I smiled at this. I had bought the Mini for her on the day she passed her driving test a couple of years earlier and she had been incredibly possessive about it from the start. I had been delighted by her jealous pleasure.

So now she was concentrating on the road and I could relax and think. We could have talked, of course, but I think we were both a little afraid. Thirty minutes under the beech trees had told us what neither of us had ever doubted, that physically nothing had changed between us. But quarrels had ended in bed before, and we knew from experience that this was the dangerous time when, lulled by a sense of universal well-being, old wounds could be probed to new inflammation. We were both too old to believe that change was ever sudden. It was enough for the moment to believe again that it was possible.

Jan broke the silence with a note of resolution in her voice.

'Listen, Harry. I'm going to tell you something. Perhaps I shouldn't. Perhaps I should wait. But it can't wait, I think. I've got to tell you now. Now at least at this moment you won't think I'm malicious. Or at least just malicious, because I don't deny malice. I can't. It would be a lie if I did.'

I lit a cigarette and recognized my need to get the props out when the emotional atmosphere became heavy. A few drops of rain curled over the windscreen but came to nothing.

'Peter came round to see me one afternoon just before you went away. He said they let him come and go as he wished at the hospital. He said he was just waiting for you to finish work so you could go on holiday.'

'He never told me this,' I said stupidly.

'No. He said he'd come to explain, to apologize. He seemed quite reasonable. I wasn't rude, not very welcoming. But not rude. Then he said that he knew from what you said that I was worried, but I needn't be. He said he was very fond of you, but just in friendship, just as a good friend. I said I was pleased to hear it, perhaps a bit sarcastically. He just laughed and said that I shouldn't believe everything I heard about him. He was quite normal really. In fact, he said, he quite fancied me.'

This is a lie, I thought in amazement. Why is she lying to me?

'He got hold of my hand. I said very starchily – you know me – that he should tell you, that in fact he could do so any minute as I was expecting you home soon (I wasn't but I was scared). This didn't stop him. If anything it seemed to please him, to excite him. I had to literally fight him off. He's not very strong, is he?'

'He's spent a lot of time in bed,' I said defensively, instinctively and, I realized at once, ridiculously.

She glanced at me with worry.

'If this is true,' I found myself saying, 'why didn't you tell me that night?'

'I might have done,' she said, 'but you rang up later to say you had some extra work to finish and you'd be going straight to the hospital from the office. I told you to go to hell. Remember?'

I remembered.

'I would have told you, I think, but by the time you got back, I'd got to like knowing that you didn't know. It gave me a real grievance to nurse. I don't think I'd had anything real up to then.'

I recognized then that she was telling the truth.

144

'Why are you telling me now?'

'To get something out of the way between us. Also, I thought, well, is it possible that Peter might have had something to do with the murders, Harry? Were you with him all the time? You said you lied to Melton to defend Peter. You're not still lying, are you? Did he really *need* defending?'

'No, no, I told the truth,' I said thoughtfully, 'I told the truth to you.'

But I was thinking now of those words of Marco's quoted to me by Melton. To make a relationship with a woman viable, Peter needed some extraordinary or dangerous circumstance. And he had found this with Jan, for a moment anyway.

'He never came back?' I asked.

'No,' she said. 'You went only a few days later. Just think, hardly a fortnight ago. But it's been worrying me this past week, Harry. I kept on thinking that Peter could do it.'

'And that was why you had doubts about me?'

'Till I saw you. Till Mam made me look at you.'

'Why did you really go home, Jan?'

She never answered the question. Out of a side lane without slowing came a police car and turned left. Jan shoved her foot hard down on the brake and we screamed to a halt. Her face flushed with anger, she blew the Mini's hysterical little horn and swore vilely. The police-car stopped and the driver got out.

Jan suddenly remembered me and our mission and took her hand off the horn. She reached for the gear lever but I gripped her hand tightly.

'Don't be daft,' I murmured. 'Be angry but don't overdo it.'

The constable leaned down till his face was level with the open window.

'What do you think you're doing?' snapped Jan. 'You of all people should look where you're going.'

'Sorry, ma'am,' said the young man equably. 'Not usually much around here at these times.'

'Well, no damage done, eh dear?' I said, smiling toothily and putting on a dreadful comic-officer accent.

'That's right, sir,' said the constable. 'You're up and about a bit early yourselves.'

'Thought we'd beat the traffic.'

'Good idea, sir. Hope you and your wife have a pleasant trip, Mr er – what did you say your name was, sir?'

'I didn't,' I said with a despairing laugh. He did not laugh back but just stood there with his face filling the tiny window. 'It's Ferguson, actually, if you must know.

'I see. Excuse me troubling you like this, Mr Ferguson, but do you have any proof of your identity. Driving licence, for instance?'

'Well no,' I said extemporizing wildly, 'lost the thing, or rather had it taken off me for a year. That's why the wife's driving.'

'You must have something, sir. Letter, library ticket. You know.'

'Doubt it,' I said. 'I travel light.' I began fishing in my pockets, avoiding my own wallet in my jacket. My fingers touched on some papers in the inside pocket of the coat. I said a prayer and pulled them out. One was an envelope. It was addressed to Ferguson.

'There's this,' I said.

He took it and turned it over two or three times, then gave it back.

'Thank you, sir. You didn't notice anyone on foot as you came along this morning, did you?'

I thought for a moment of describing myself about five miles back, but at once dismissed the idea as stupid.

'No, we didn't. Anything up?'

'Nothing to bother you, sir. Ma'am.'

He touched his cap and went back to the car.

We watched him out of sight.

'That was quick thinking,' said Jan.

146

'Not a bit of it. It was the only name I could think of apart from my own.'

'I wonder what little Annie's up to today,' said Jan, casually.

I ignored her and put Ferguson's envelope away and then glanced at the other papers I had pulled out with it. They were the notes and jottings Will had handed me to study that morning. I shivered at how close I'd been to handing them to the policeman and wondered what he would have made of them if I had. I glanced at Jan, but she was now really concentrating on her driving. We couldn't afford any accidents even if they weren't with police cars.

I began to study Will's bits of paper. He'd really done a quite remarkable job though as I glanced down the orderly list before me, I realized that it was really just a systematical presentation of the information and alternatives offered by all the newspaper reports he had read. There were the usual discrepancies from one paper to another, the result of imagination in some cases and indolence in others.

I folded it up and put it in my pocket, then looked at Will's notes on my own account of the fatal day. Again his orderly mind was very much in evidence. The events of that day again ran through my mind as I read and in the end I shook away the memory and put the paper with the other.

But then something nagged in a corner of my mind. It was like one of those times when you turn the page of a newspaper and suddenly know you've caught a glimpse of a certain word on the page you are turning. You may have to search for ages to find it (if such things bother you; they do me) and sometimes you find it wasn't the word you thought at all, but a couple of words which together form something like it.

I took the papers out again and after much searching, I found it. I looked at my discovery in disappointment. It was like the bit of grit in your eye which, once removed, looks minute. I sat and studied for a while. Insignificant it might be, but it was all there was.

'Look,' said Jan, 'we're nearly on the A6.'

'Pull up,' I said.

'Why?'

'Just pull up.'

The car rolled to a stop and Jan turned off the engine.

'Well?'

'You've got to go back to Thurbeck and see your father.'

'What! Are you mad?'

'No. Take this paper and ask him why he wrote this.' I underlined an item with my nail.

Jan peered down at the list.

'What's the idea? I don't get you.'

'Just ask him.'

'And what are you going to do?'

'It'd be silly for me to take the risk of being seen again. I'll wait.'

She laughed.

'Just wait? By the roadside? As if for a bus?'

I shook my head and pointed across the field to our left.

'See those trees. I'll shin up one of them and watch for you coming back. Then nip back across the field, hop in, and we're no worse off than before, are we?'

Jan stared at me distrustingly.

'This isn't some kind of brush-off, is it, Harry? For chivalrous or other reasons? You're not just going to take off into the blue the minute I'm out of sight, are you?'

'Don't be stupid,' I said. 'Even if I wanted to, which I don't, wouldn't I wait till you'd driven me somewhere a bit more civilized than this?'

'I suppose so,' she said doubtfully.

'Perhaps you think that that's just a Machiavellian twist to throw you off the scent,' I said with heavy sarcasm, getting out of the car.

She seized my hand and hung on to it for a moment. Then, 'Look after yourself, Superboy,' she said, and spun the Mini into an exhibitionistic three-point turn.

I watched her out of sight then set off cautiously across

the field. Shinning up the tree was harder to do than to say, but somehow I managed it. As I sat in great discomfort in a fork which seemed to be gripping me tighter and tighter like a pair of pincers, I vowed to discard forever the boyhood memories of happy hours spent dreaming green dreams sixty feet up.

It was still very early and there was next to no traffic on this small side-road. A farm tractor went by after about ten minutes, then there was nothing for half an hour, when I saw with some unease a police car drive slowly along. I couldn't make out if it was the same one that had nearly crashed with us earlier. But it passed out of sight without slowing down and a few minutes later I saw it pass round a curve in the road about a quarter of a mile away and just visible from my perch.

I relaxed again and resumed my vigil for Jan. The powers of patience I had so recently congratulated myself on developing had got lost somewhere and I was as nervous and fidgety as my precarious position would permit. I told myself a hundred times that a single figure could not possibly have any significance at all – for that was all I had underlined with my thumb-nail.

The item had read: '2: climb down gully to sheep.' It was the 2 I was interested in. Was it just Will's way of tabulating the items? Or was it perhaps a time? If it *was* a time, I thought . . . but what if it was? There were a thousand explanations.

There was only one which interested me.

I shifted again and a thrush which had finally plucked up courage to settle in what was obviously his own personal tree rose up again, his speckles heaving with indignation.

In the distance there was a flash. Sun on a windscreen? I was right. The blue Mini came terrier-like along the road.

I nearly broke my leg dropping out of that tree and hobbled across the field, bending low for token concealment.

'Come on, Quasimodo,' said Jan. I literally hopped into the car and we set off almost before the door closed.

'What's the hurry?' I asked.

'It's pointless hanging about. We'll just draw attention to ourselves. That police car's still prowling about.'

'Yes, I saw it.'

'So did I. I just hope they didn't have time to realize this was the same car as before – minus one male passenger.'

We screeched round a corner, if not on two wheels, then at least with the outside pair on tiptoe.

'For God's sake!' I cried.

'Take it easy,' she said, 'you haven't fastened your seatbelt.'

I did so at once.

'Well,' I said.

'What?'

'What did Will say?'

'Hang on.'

We turned another corner and tore along a straight, slowing as we passed a sign saying 'Halt – major road ahead.'

It was the A6. Right lay Penrith and the south; left was Carlisle.

We seemed to be approaching very quickly if we were going to cut right across the road.

'Watch it,' I said warningly.

Jan said nothing, but glanced to her right as we reached the junction, and swung the wheel over hard left.

'What in the name!' I expostulated. 'What are you doing?'

As we were now on a broad straight main road with excellent visibility, Jan slowed down to a steady sedate pace.

'Dad said he wrote 2 because that was the time Peter went after the sheep. He backtracked a bit and found that he had not got the time from you as he thought when I first asked him, but he'd got it indirectly from one of the newspapers.'

'Which one? What did it say?'

'It was the local paper, as it happens. It had an interview with the boys from the Wyrton Boys' Club, the ones who

150

saw you with the girls. Here's the paper, I've ringed the bit.'

She passed me a cutting headlined, with great verve I thought, 'Wyrton Boys Help Police.' Now if it had been the *Mirror*, there would have been something about the Sun Shining on Murder Mountain.

The paragraph ringed read simply, 'Alan Hayhurst, 15, the youngest of the group, showed the binoculars through which he had his last glimpse of the murdered girls. "It was about 2 o'clock," he said, "and we were just getting ready to move on again after having our sandwiches. I looked all around the fells and then I noticed the two girls."'

They had kept well away from any identification of us in the paper. As it was, I thought they were sailing a bit near the wind in talking to witnesses of this age. But it might be of some help to me so I had no cause to be censorious.

Yet now I had the source of that mysterious 2 in my hands, I could not see how it could really help.

'The thing is,' I began to Jan.

'The thing is, it was well before two when you met the girls and you want to know who it was who was with them *at* two.'

'Right. But perhaps it's just a misprint, or a misunderstanding. Or his watch was wrong. What can I do about it anyway? And why are we heading towards Carlisle. London, in case you've forgotten, is south.'

'And Wyrton, a small but thriving village, is approximately two miles north of Carlisle.'

I threw up my hands in mock admiration.

'My! Aren't you and Will the smart ones! What am I supposed to do there anyway! Walk up to whatsisname – Alan Hayhurst's house and say "Excuse me, Mrs Hayhurst, but can I speak to your son, Alan. My name is Bentink and he mistakenly thinks he saw me with those poor murdered girls at two p.m. on the fatal day." She'll let me in, of course.'

'What's happened to Superboy?' asked Jan. 'You will find a way.'

151

'Of course, it would be different if *you* went and did the talking, dear,' I said speculatively.

'I told you you'd find a way,' she said.

It was too early for the customary traffic jam to have built up in Carlisle and we crossed the city boundary at an illegal fifty.

'Steady,' I said, partly because of the speed limit and partly because the car was bumping and bouncing over a series of ridges and potholes.

'I see now why they like traffic jams here,' said Jan, slowing to thirty, 'they stop you noticing the state of the road.'

I laughed, then thought ruefully to myself that we hadn't laughed together like this for a long time. What would happen to us when the impetus of the now strangely exhilarating circumstances wore off? I wondered if we would slow down to the old grinding speed. I knew our marriage was not a vehicle which could survive bottom gear for long – we were not made for mere tolerance of each other. Of course, the strangely exhilarating circumstances might never end – for me. I felt certain deep inside that we were on a wild goose-chase. The chances of the report of the time being accurate seemed very long, the more I thought about it. The identification of us had been positive. At least, Melton said it had been positive. I sat up straight at the thought and poked my head against the roof. Melton – I had no idea what the boys had really told him. Perhaps it had been much vaguer. Perhaps, the more sinisterly, they had been subtly persuaded into a positive identification. If Copley had talked to them, I could easily believe it. My doubts were resolved. I had to see those boys.

Something of my indecision must have shown for Jan glanced at me and said, 'Well. What's the plan?'

We were approaching the centre of the city through a dark industrial canyon. This broadened out eventually into a shopping area which in turn broadened into the station square.

152

'Find a hotel,' I said.

'Big, little, scruffy, temperance?' she asked.

'Big,' I said. 'They're more easily impressed. We can't just hang about the place, it attracts too much attention. We've got to have a base.'

'Right,' she said, and we pulled to a halt in front of a not inelegant building which had a sign in Gothic script advertising that we were arriving at the Carliol.

We were welcomingly received at reception and with surprising lack of fuss for an English hotel so early in the morning (it was still only nine-thirty) were taken to our room immediately. I repeated my patter about starting early to avoid the traffic and was assured that this was a splendid idea. I decided to push my luck even further and enquired diffidently about breakfast.

'Certainly, sir,' said the girl from the reception desk, who was herself leading us upstairs.

'Would you like it in your room or will you come down?'

'In our room,' said Jan with a honeymooner's simper.

'I'll send a waiter up,' the receptionist replied with a smile, opening a bedroom door. 'Here we are.'

We sat down and laughed together when she had gone. I reached over and took Jan in my arms. There was a sharp knock at the door. We sprang apart like adulterers.

'Come in,' I said.

It was the waiter. The sight of him brought Peter to my mind and I knew that here was another problem which I had merely shelved for the moment.

When the waiter had taken our order and gone I said to Jan, 'By the way, I hope you've got some money. With this kind of service the bill must be astronomical.'

'I've got enough,' said Jan. 'I haven't exactly been able to spend much in the last few days.'

'You'll spend a bit more in a while,' I said. 'They're looking for me in a brown suit, and I can't wear Ferguson's coat all day. It's going to be warm again as well.'

'Right. Then what?'

'This is how I see it. We idle away this morning. Then this afternoon we head out to Wyrton. I drop out at the edge of the village. You go on to this Hayhurst child's house, say you're a reporter, writer, sociologist, anything. But get talking to him and check on this time business.'

'And if he sticks to two p.m.?'

'Then get a description, find out exactly what he saw, try to see if any pressure has been brought to bear on him by the police.'

'And then?'

'I don't know. I don't know. If he does say two then it wasn't me and Peter. That's all. There were five of those boys altogether, weren't there?'

'Six.'

'Six. Right. And they all looked through the binoculars, so Melton said anyway. But he could have been lying. But if he wasn't, then surely six of them couldn't mistake someone else for us. There must have been some difference of clothing or something.'

I must have been talking rather loudly for Jan put a restraining hand on my arm.

'Take it easy, Harry. That, to me, just makes it more likely that there's been a mistake about the time.'

I nodded reluctantly.

'Yes. I suppose so.'

There came another knock on the door and our breakfast was brought in. It lived up to the standard of service which had produced it and I felt quite bloated by the time I had finished. I lounged on the bed and sent Jan out to do some shopping. Forecastably I was asleep when she returned an hour later.

She had brought me a casual sweater and a pair of slacks.

'Marks and Sparks,' she said. 'I didn't want to risk getting a jacket, it might have looked odd. I hope these fit. You look as if you've lost a bit of weight.'

'Ah, it's this athletic life I've been leading,' I said. 'Let's see.'

154

The slacks did in fact need tightening to the last notch despite the huge breakfast I had just eaten. I looked at myself in the mirror and was quite content with the lack of resemblance to any photograph of myself I had ever seen. The last touch was a straw Panama which Jan set on the back of my head.

'How do I look?' I asked, preening myself. 'Like the major on leave?'

'No,' she said, 'more like a used car salesman trying to look like the major on leave. Here, I got something else.'

She produced one of those little leather holders with plastic tops in which people keep season tickets and the like. Out of her handbag she took a piece of white card and a black felt-tip pen. Her tongue curled round her teeth in concentration, she worked on the card for a few moments then, satisfied at last, showed it to me. It said in large bold capitals PRESS, then in smaller letters underneath, *The Observer*, and underneath this in blue ink she had signed her maiden name.

'What is it?' I asked.

'It's my press card,' she said, slipping it into the holder.

'Is that what they look like?' I said.

'I don't know. I've never seen one. Have you?'

'Not till this very minute.'

'Come on then,' she said. 'We can't hang around here all morning or they'll wonder about us.'

'We could have pretended we were on our honeymoon.'

'Then we'd have skipped breakfast. I wouldn't have missed that.'

We went out into the town like any holiday couple. I had only passed through the place before, both by rail and road, and I was pleased to find it so much more pleasant than such experiences had indicated. Jan knew it quite well. It had been the great metropolis to her when a child. Old Will had thought it was pretty near hell, so full it was of people and cars and noise, so Jan's visits had not been all that frequent.

155

Neither of us wanted any lunch. We had both breakfasted well, of course, but it was also a nervousness in the gut which kept hunger from us. It was a kind of nervousness I had not yet felt, though I had felt fear often enough of late. But this was the feeling which came from our awareness that if nothing came from our trip to Wyrton (and what *could* come of it? I asked myself agonizedly for the hundredth time) then all we could do was to head for some larger city and hide and hope that something would turn up which would prove my innocence. I could always take a chance with a jury, I thought, but discarded the idea immediately. I would rather keep this restricted freedom I had than risk losing it also. Jan, of course, could show herself when she wanted. But it was certain once she did so that Melton would not let her out of his sight again.

The joy of the morning went with these thoughts and the afternoon found us driving north out of the city in solemn mood.

On the northern outskirts where the road forked left to Glasgow, right to Edinburgh, we took the left-hand fork and kept on the main road for about a mile and a half before turning off. A few minutes later we stopped. Ahead of us lay signs of habitation, a couple of farmhouses, and the roofs of more just a little behind them.

'What's it to be this time?' asked Jan. 'Are you going up a tree again?'

'No,' I said. 'I'll just take a little stroll up through that wood. Come and look for me if you can't see me.'

'Right.'

'Good luck, Jan,' I said, and kissed her.

The wood was not very extensive; obviously a triangular survival from the distant days when all that area had been heavily wooded. But it was deep enough for me. The trees were mainly beech with a few birch bright as candles among them. The ground was firm underfoot, though springy with moss. I saw a grey squirrel hop lethargically up a tree. A cabbage-white made its erratic way between the branches

156

which moved with the slowness of the green weed on the bed of a lake.

I sat down on an old log and tried to submerge myself in the moment, in the single place I was. But the moment and the place were not deep enough to cover my restless mind.

Then Jan came up behind me. I did not notice her, so concerned with my thoughts was I, and started when she spoke.

'Nothing yet. He's not in. His mother says he'll be back at tea-time, and I've sweet-talked her into letting me see him.'

I was ill with disappointment. But at least this last puny little card was still mine to play.

Jan sat down beside me and gave me a cigarette. I realized with surprise that I had been smoking considerably less lately and wondered if I could give them up altogether.

'I think I'll give up,' I said. Jan looked at me anxiously and I realized she thought I was referring to our plans. Or to myself.

'Smoking. But you'll have to give it up too.'

'Why?'

'I can't bear women whose breath tastes of tobacco.'

She laughed.

'Harry. Seriously, what's going to happen to us when this is over? Have you thought? I mean, since last night, it's been good to be with you. But what are we now, Harry? What's really left to us when this is done?'

Her words so closely echoed my thoughts that at first I gave her the reply of silence which was all I had been able to give myself.

'I don't know,' I said finally. 'I can't imagine myself ever being the same again. Not now. Not after this.'

'It's me as well,' she said. 'I have to change too.'

She looked at me seriously as she spoke. It was no mere gesture of concession.

'The trouble is,' I replied, 'all this, it's so impermanent. The situation, I mean. Perhaps what we feel too. I wish

157

there were some way of knowing. The truth, I mean, about oneself, and telling someone else. Perhaps your dad's got the right idea. Sit down with pen and paper and write it all down till you see what you're getting at.'

'Perhaps he has,' said Jan. 'You try it. But writing's a lonely business. You're not alone now. There are other ways of trying to tell.'

I reached over and took her in my arms and we said very little for the next half hour. I could have rested like that much longer, but finally Jan disengaged herself and looked at her watch.

'I'd better go and try young Alan again. Won't be long.'

'Don't,' I said, 'somehow it doesn't seem quite so important now.'

'No.' She started to walk away, then stopped and turned. 'Harry.'

'Yes.'

'I've got to ask. This girl, Annie Ferguson. Is she competition?'

'Not really. I don't know. She might have been. But she's got a father. Strong, attractive, bearded.'

'She told you to shave.'

'A condemnation.'

'Or an invitation. Perhaps she's turning over a new leaf.'

'It will have to be in someone else's book.'

She smiled and made to turn again, but I stopped her.

'Now you tell me. Why did you visit your parents?'

'Now, where else should an affected, insecure, guilt-ridden, snobbish, pretentious, unique daughter go but to her parents? I was lonely. I wanted to find someone who loved me.'

She went away swiftly then and I cursed myself for the damage I had done to her without my knowledge.

This time she was away much longer and evening was drawing on when she returned. I leapt up at her approach.

'Anything?' I asked eagerly.

She sank down beside me.

'I'm not sure,' she said thoughtfully. 'I can't make it out. But there does seem to be something a bit odd. I talked to the boy and he seemed quite willing to talk to me. I asked him about various things, then finally I asked him about the time when he used his binoculars, and he said two o'clock. No hesitation, right out, absolutely precise. I sort of laughed and asked how he could be so sure of the time and he said he looked at his watch. He had it on, a good solid, reliable, boy's watch it looked. Then I asked what he saw. He demurred a bit here, saying the police had told him to be careful of what he said, but I explained that my editor couldn't print anything the police wouldn't like anyway. His mother, who was obviously relishing her own vicarious fame no end, urged him on, and he then gave a most graphic description of you and Peter.'

I sighed in disappointment.

'Well, that's that. It must have been his watch.'

'No, hang on a minute. I came back to this business about the time when I realized how exactly his description tallied with your clothes and features. And he insisted it was two. Now there was another boy there for tea, Colin something who'd been one of the party, and he supported Alan vehemently, saying he'd looked at his watch as well and it was dead on two. I asked him if he'd looked through the glasses and he said he had. Then he described you and Peter as well.'

I shrugged.

'I don't know,' I said helplessly. 'Perhaps I was mistaken. Perhaps my watch was wrong, though I never noticed any discrepancy later.'

'I'm not finished yet, Harry. I noticed something rather odd. Or at least it seemed a bit odd when I thought about it. This was the precise way in which they both described you and Peter.'

'Well, they had seen us in the bar the previous night and on the fells only a couple of hours earlier that day.'

'I know. I thought of that. But it was more than that.

159

There were distinct verbal echoes between them. And the order in which they mentioned things was almost exactly the same in both cases.'

I sat up at this.

'You mean you think they'd been rehearsed?'

'I don't know. How does it sound to you?' I sat in thought, running over in my mind all I could recollect of my few hours' acquaintance with Melton.

'Melton, no, I don't think so,' I said finally. 'In fact, I'd say not, surely. But there was this other chap, this Inspector Copley, you'll remember I mentioned him last night. Now he was a very different proposition, I think. Or at least he was made out to be so. I'm not sure how much of it was a double act. But it could be. It could be. Yet it still doesn't explain the time. Copley might have reinforced their memory of what they saw at a great distance, but why this time factor? Could he have convinced them that they saw us when it was really someone else? Where's that newspaper cutting?'

She dug around in her bag and finally produced it. I scanned through it quickly, stopping when I came to a sentence which referred to 'the leader of the party, eighteen-year-old Sam Cooper.' The open face and blond hair rose into my mind's eye.

'That's the one I want to see,' I said. 'He's the one I'd like to talk to. He'll sort things out.'

'How do we get to him?'

I smiled at her.

'The same as before to start with. His address isn't in the report, so you'll have to use your journalistic skill and ferret it out.'

'And what do I do when I find him? He'll just repeat the same story as the youngsters, that is if he talks to me at all.'

'Well, just see how much the same it is. See if there's any really indicative similarity of phrasing or anything else. It's very likely if the other two are close friends that their descriptions sound the same purely because they've been

160

over it all so many times in each others' company We need a third witness just for comparison.'

'And if you think that Copley has got at them. What then?'

'I don't know. See if you can get a hint of this lad's movements tonight. I'd like a word with him myself.'

Jan looked worried.

'Wouldn't that be foolish? It would really pinpoint your position.'

'They don't know I've got transport. Or you.'

But she still wasn't happy.

'It'll only take a couple of questions for the police to connect a bogus female reporter with you.'

'They don't know you're bogus.'

'A couple of telephone calls to check will soon reveal *that*. Your lad is bound to mention me.'

I could see the complete validity of all her arguments, but I was like a terrier now with his prey between his teeth. I wasn't going to stop worrying it till it was dead.

'All right,' I said. 'I'll think about it. But there's no harm in you going and chatting him up if you can find him. At least that will give us a bit more to go on.'

'Right,' she replied, and rose once more. 'Here we go again.'

She set off through the trees and I settled down for another long wait. But within minutes Jan was back by my side.

'Harry,' she panted, 'there's a policeman at my car.'

I leapt to my feet and smoothly swept her behind a tree, where I crouched down and peered toward the edge of the wood. I was hardly conscious of doing this, so used does the human mind become even to being hunted, but there must have been something ludicrously efficient about my movement for Jan giggled and murmured, 'Shades of Fenimore Cooper!'

I deliberately did not share her amusement, but asked, 'What's he doing?'

161

'He was peering into the thing and I think he had his note-book out. It must have been very lucky that he even saw it. I'd parked it well off the road behind a couple of bushes.'

'Lucky? Not for us. What kind of policeman is he?'

'What kind? I don't know. He might be the big, fat, red-faced jolly kind always ready to help . . .'

'Is he the local constable with tall hat and pushbike. Or is he a flat-hatted Z-car copper?'

'Oh, I see. Oh, the first, definitely. He looks very slow and very thorough. Will it matter, do you think? I mean, he's probably been dying to get something down in his book all week and an empty car is the only event of interest which he's come across. And can we get up from here? This tree is very abrasive and I'm getting cramp.'

'Stay here,' I ordered, and set off, crouched low, through the trees, dropping on to all fours as the wood began to thin out.

I looked across to the road but I could not even see the car let alone the policeman. There was no sign of any kind of life. I returned to Jan with the same care. She was leaning up against the tree with a newly-lit cigarette in her mouth. I took it from her, took a long draw and stubbed it out.

'Damn,' I said. 'This makes things difficult.'

'Why? There must be any number of unattended cars left parked in odd places all over the country.'

'I know. It might mean nothing. It depends what he does now. Suppose he keeps an eye on it? Suppose he checks the licence number and thinks it interesting that it belongs to a Mrs Janet Bentink? Suppose that policeman who stopped us this morning has done the same?'

'You can suppose every disaster under the sun, if you like. What's important is what do we do now? Do we wait till the coast is clear, get back into the car and head out of here, hell for leather? Or do we carry on with our original plan?'

I shrugged my shoulders.

'There's little choice. If he is going to check up on the car, then we'd be stopped in a short while anyway. So we might as well proceed with the plan. But make sure he's well out of the way. He'd probably want a very much closer look at that Press card than the local yokels.'

'Your wish is my command,' said Janet, and set off once again, this time crouched ludicrously low and moving with exaggerated stealth. I laughed to myself as I watched. She turned and waved with absurd caution then disappeared.

It was full dark when she returned. I heard her stumbling through the undergrowth and whispering my name.

'Here!' I hissed in reply. She fell into my arms.

'I thought I was never going to find you. Come on, darling. We've got to go. You were right.'

'What's happened?'

She was tugging me towards the edge of the wood as she spoke.

'They must have checked the car or something, I don't know. But a couple of police cars pulled up in front of the village station as I was coming out. Something's up and it's probably us.'

'Did they see you?' I asked urgently.

'Of course not!' She sounded indignant.

'And where's the car? Not in the same place as before, I hope!'

She punched me in the ribs.

'Do you think I'm stupid? Come on. I've got it parked much further along this time and really well hidden. Let's MOVE!'

'Wait,' I said. 'You haven't told me about Sam Cooper.'

'In the car,' she urged, but I was adamant. I stopped dead and easily resisted her attempts to drag me along by main force.

'Now. I must know now.'

'For God's sake. All right. Yes, it was the same as before. Not quite so obvious, he's no mere kid. But obviously they've been got at by someone.'

'Copley,' I said viciously. 'It's got to be that bastard.'

163

'Will you come now?'

I let myself be dragged a few paces, then stopped again.

'No,' I said.

'What?'

'No,' I repeated. 'I'm not coming. Look, at the moment it's the car they must be after, if they are after anything at all, and we still don't know that for sure.'

'Oh no,' she said, 'perhaps a dozen policemen all live together in that little house.'

'All right. So it's probably us. Or rather you. Or rather the car. They're bound to stop it pretty soon, so what's the point of me being in it?'

'OK then. Where do we go and how? On foot?'

'No. Not "we". Me. You go and get the car. If they find that empty, they'll start a full-scale search round here. You take off in the car and give them a run for their money. When they stop you, be indignant. You've been by yourself all day. Admit you've been out here. Play the plucky little wife trying to prove her husband innocent.'

'And what will *you* be doing?'

'Me? I'll be all right.'

'You're going to talk to that youth, aren't you?'

I saw no point in denying it.

'Yes.'

'What then?'

'Then at least I'll know what I'm up against. If I can only get him to admit that Copley has bullied, or bribed, or brainwashed him . . .'

'And the other five.'

'And the other five. OK, so it sounds unlikely. But it must have happened. And I've got to find out what they really saw. If I manage to get away, I'll get in touch.'

'How?'

'I'll telephone.'

'You'd better hurry now or they'll be waiting for you at the car.'

'It's well hidden, I tell you.'

164

She hugged me close to her.

'Take care of yourself, Harry. I hate leaving you like this.'

She faded away among the trees. It was only after she disappeared completely from view that I realized I had forgotten to ask her where I would find Cooper. I cursed, but then thought that the village did not seem all that big. If he was out at all, I should be able to spot him. But first I had to make sure the police were out of the way.

Despite the fact that it was a dark overcast night, I made my way with remarkable ease and silence back to the road. My mood of mild self-congratulation almost caused me to walk into a couple of policemen who were having a quiet cigarette before returning to report that the car was no longer there. At least this is what I surmised as I lay in the ditch where I had dropped as soon as I saw them.

They finally set off up the road to where they had left their own car and I saw them start up and head back into the village. I lay where I was a little longer, which was just as well, for suddenly with a roar of engines and a glare of headlights, two cars came racing from the village and speeded past me with lights flashing and bells ringing.

I smiled to myself. Someone had spotted Jan. The chase was on.

I studied the village closely from a vantage point among some trees which lined the road right up to the first house. It was bigger than I had thought, and the recent police activity was mirrored in a greater activity in the streets than I felt was normal. Not that I dared risk showing myself, of course. The place was not so large that every one of its inhabitants would not know everyone else by sight, if not by name. So I just stood behind my tree and watched. Soon the street was almost empty except for the occasional figure moving purposefully along towards the small pub which fitted in so well with the houses on either side, that only a small printed legend over the door informed the noninitiate that here was an inn. I was just about to take the risk of penetrating further into the village when a door opened in a house which was almost at the extreme point of my vision, and out into the street stepped a youth whom I recognized even at that distance as the blond boy I had seen in the Derwent Hotel. Cooper.

He moved quickly over the few yards which separated his front door from the pub and went in. I looked at my watch. It was still over an hour to closing time. I did not dare go in after him, but neither did I fancy hanging about here for much longer. I debated working on the assumption that he was going to be inside till closing time and finding myself a more secure retreat for an hour. But fortunately I was still weighing the pros and cons of this ten minutes later when the pub door opened and Cooper came out again accompanied by another youth.

They set off up the street away from me. When they were almost round the bend out of sight, I threw caution to the winds, pulled my hat down over my brow, and set off after them.

They did not go far, but soon turned off up a steep cobbled path which I could see, even before I reached it, led up towards the church.

But the church itself was obviously not their goal, I realized as I rounded the corner. Alongside it, separated from it only by a narrow strip of graveyard and an ancient wall, was what I took to be the village hall. It was a squat, plain, functional looking building in contrast with the rather pretty sandstone-built church. The small-paned windows were lit up and the two boys were just entering as I turned the corner.

I myself went quietly through the church gate into the graveyard and strode across the rounded graves with scant regard for either religion or superstition, till I reached the old wall. Some headstones obviously of great antiquity had been moved up against it, probably to make way for others. Even in death the jostling of the generations does not end.

I used one as a step and first removing my hat, out of caution, not respect, I raised my head slowly over the top of the wall.

I could see quite clearly through the uncurtained windows into the hall. Some kind of meeting was taking place of what I assumed was the Wyrton Boys' Club. They were being addressed by a rather brutal-looking cleric. There were about a dozen or perhaps fifteen boys there, of all ages from about thirteen on. Cooper and his friend, obviously the oldest, sat at the back looking rather superior. I suppose they were at the age where the power of being the oldest in such an organization had to be balanced carefully against the possible indignity of being classed with the young. Still, I thought, at least Sam Cooper had taken a party from the club on holiday and, unless I was mistaken, his companion had been in the group also.

The vicar came to an end, there was a bit of discussion, then he looked at his watch, clapped his hands together once and obviously declared the meeting closed. Chairs and tables were rearranged in some kind of order while the vicar made his way to the back and had a chat with the late-comers. Whether he reprimanded them or not was impossible to tell, but he certainly left them amicably enough, clapping Cooper on the shoulder and saying, I felt certain, that he knew he could rely on Sam to see that things were left tidy. He then left. Cooper and his friend grinned at each other as the door closed behind him. But they justified his confidence for the place was ship-shape in no time and the boys began drifting away. I did not see any commands or requests given, but after a few minutes the drifting stopped and only the two older youths and four others remained. I could have made no positive identification apart from Cooper himself, but I knew for certain in my mind that these were the six on the mountain.

They stood around uncertainly except for Cooper, who sat nonchalantly astride a chair, and his lieutenant, who stood behind him. Cooper appeared to be asking one of the boys some questions. Alan Hayhurst? I wondered. Then, apparently satisfied, he grinned at them, said something which made his crony laugh heartily but only brought uneasy smiles to the faces of the others, then dismissed them with a wave.

Soon there were only the two of them there. I prayed that the other lad might go also, leaving Cooper on his own, but this was obviously unlikely to happen. And when they both began moving to the door, I knew I had to act. I doubted whether I'd get a better opportunity than this, and though I did not like having to face two of them, particularly if they decided to be heroic and 'catch the murderer', I thought there might be some profit in it if, as I felt certain, Cooper's companion was also a witness against me.

I scrambled over the wall and quickly made my way round to the door. It opened as I arrived and Cooper stood there. He was looking back over his shoulder, saying something, and he started violently when he turned and saw me before him.

I stepped forward into the doorway.

'Let's go back inside and talk,' I said, and kicked the door shut behind me.

'Light!' I commanded. The second youth reached out and turned the lights on again. We stood and faced each other.

It says much for the effect of my moustache and Ferguson's hat that Cooper had to stare at me for a full minute before even the suspicion of who I was began to cloud his eyes.

'Yes, Sam,' I said. 'I'm Bentink. Harry Bentink. You recognized me easier a quarter of a mile away through binoculars than you did now. Long-sighted, are we?'

He looked a little pale, but his voice was very steady when he spoke.

'What do you want, Mr Bentink?' he asked respectfully.

I looked at him thoughtfully. I still hadn't decided on the best approach. But bullying was out, I thought, studying his quiet demeanour.

'Let's sit down, shall we?' I said finally, and planted

168

myself on a chair. After a second, he followed suit, not sitting astride now, but very upright and formally, almost on the edge.

'And your friend?' I asked.

'Mervyn. Sit down, Merv.'

Mervyn was very obviously nervous and sat down a few yards away from Cooper and myself, who sat about a yard apart, facing each other.

'Sam,' I said. 'Let's get one thing straight. I didn't kill those girls. So I haven't come here to shut up witnesses, get revenge, or anything like that. You understand me?'

'Yes, sir,' he said.

'Do you believe me?'

'Well, I don't know,' he said uncertainly.

I interrupted. 'Of course, you can't say. I'm sorry. It was a silly question. But you realize, of course, that the evidence of you and your friends is very strong evidence against me?'

'Yes, sir.'

'So you must be quite sure that what you say is true, Sam. Not what you might have seen, not what someone has told you you might have seen, but what you *did* see.'

'Yes.'

'Did you look through the binoculars, Sam?'

'Yes, I did.'

'And you, Mervyn.'

Mervyn was becoming more and more nervous and was possibly contemplating making a dash for it and getting help. I doubt if I could have stopped him.

'Answer Mr Bentink, Merv.'

He looked at Cooper, then nodded and said very quickly, 'Yes, I looked through the binoculars third and I saw you and . . .'

'Never mind what you saw for the moment. What time was it that you looked through the binoculars? Do you know?'

Cooper looked at me appraisingly but Mervyn burst out

without hesitation, 'It was just two o'clock, I know because I looked at my watch.'

'And you, Sam? What do you say?'

'Why do you ask, Mr Bentink?'

I decided to put my cards on the table. He seemed an intelligent youth. He also seemed almost to co-operate, which I found rather strange. But I was in no position to refuse any straw sent me to clutch at.

'Look, Sam, my friend, Mr Thorne, and I did meet those girls on the mountain, we don't deny it. But when we met them, it was definitely before one o'clock. So if you saw them alive at two with a couple of men, then it must have been someone else. This is what I want to find out. Who was with them? I know it wasn't us. Now, if you say it was us, you're mistaken, or you've had the idea planted in your heads.'

'What do you mean?'

'Has someone got at you? Did someone suggest that it must have been us, because they'd got so much other evidence against us? Is this what happened? Were the words put into your mouth? Was it Copley?'

I had not meant to go this far, but I was more wrought up than I had realized. But Sam's reply came like a douche of cold water.

'Who's Copley, Mr Bentink?'

'Inspector Copley of the police. One of the officers in charge,' I said dully.

'I don't think we met him. Did we, Merv?'

Mervyn shook his head in an affirmative negative.

'Think again, Sam,' I urged. 'What did these men you saw look like? There must have been something distinctive about them.'

'Oh there was, Mr Bentink. They looked just like you and Mr Thorne.'

I sat back in resignation. Sam leaned forward and said in a solicitous tone, 'What time did you say you met the girls, Mr Bentink?'

'About one o'clock.'

'About one. We might have made a mistake about the time, mightn't we, Mervyn? It might have been about one, not two after all.'

I was so sunk in disappointment that only dimly did this remark penetrate my mind, but as it began to sink in and as I slowly realized that this willingness to change the time was not just a contradiction of what one boy had said, but a contradiction of what at least three boys (all looking at their watches) had said. Indeed, a contradiction of what the whole six, including Cooper, had said.

I think it was then that the monstrous suspicion turned over once in my mind and was still.

But I had felt it turn. I got up and took a couple of steps towards the door, then stopped and faced them again.

Cooper stood up also.

'I'm very sorry we couldn't help you, Mr Bentink.'

He was too damned respectful to a man whom he was going to help condemn.

'You're quite certain, are you, Sam,' I said pleadingly, 'that it was Mr Thorne and myself you saw on Great End with the girls?'

'I'm sorry. Yes, it was. We must have been wrong about the time.'

'You must have been on your way up Scafell Pike then to look across at Great End.' Casually.

He looked thoughtful for a moment, then nodded.

'Yes, that's right.'

My monstrous suspicion was now heaving its back and stretching its legs. Soon it would be wanting to move out into the daylight.

'Tell me, Mervyn,' I said suddenly. 'Which of us had his jacket on, Mr Thorne or myself?'

Mervyn looked the picture of utter confusion, but opened his mouth to answer, only to be interrupted by Sam's sharp, 'Neither!'

171

'That's right,' I said. 'I forgot. You saw us earlier near the tarn, didn't you?'

Sam moved towards me.

'What are you getting at, Mr Bentink?'

I thought I might as well go all the way as I had nothing to lose. I did not know how wrong I was.

I smiled knowingly.

'I think you know what I'm getting at, Sam. You had a visitor today, didn't you? A woman.'

'Yes.'

'You didn't tell her much, did you? You're a close one, Sam. But young Hayhurst isn't so clever. She talked to him as well.'

'Who was she?' He had a look of mild interest on his face. We might have been friends chatting at a street corner.

'She was my wife, Sam.'

'And?'

'And what young Hayhurst told her has made us very suspicious.'

'Of what?'

I laughed, thinking what a ham actor I sounded to myself.

'You don't want me to say it, Sam. *You* know what I mean, Mervyn.'

I wasn't sure I knew what I meant myself. Or perhaps whether I meant what I meant. But Mervyn's face, white and loose, made me go on.

'I just came here to get confirmation. You made a mistake, Sam. I was never on Great End that day. Never.'

If I thought this was a trump card, I was mistaken. Cooper just looked at me thoughtfully for a moment, then shook his head sadly.

'I don't know the names of all these mountains, Mr Bentink. I hardly know what mountain I was on myself. If you say you were on Great End, why, I believe you. If you say you were on another fell, then I believe that. I don't see what you're making so much fuss about.'

172

I knew when I was beaten, but I kept a bright look on my face. I was sure my father had said something about situations like this but I couldn't remember what.

'I'm off then,' I said cheerily. 'Don't bother to ring the police. I'm going straight along to Superintendent Melton anyway.'

It was a pathetic enough finale. Cooper raised one eyebrow sardonically at me. I turned and made for the door.

I wasn't going for the police, of course. I did not even know whether to give any credence at all to my own suspicions. I certainly could see no way of getting anyone else to take notice of them. In fact, as my hand was on the door knob, I was already contemplating possible routes to London.

But as I pulled the door open there was a scuffle behind me, I heard Mervyn's voice say, 'You can't let him go,' and Cooper's at the same time. 'Wait, you fool!' and then there were footsteps behind me.

I turned in time to see Mervyn, face twisted with fear, bearing down on me. Behind him, his face twisted with anger, was Sam. One other thing I noticed. Mervyn clutched a chair in his hands. I flung my hands up too late to do anything but faintly deflect the blow as he brought it crashing down on my head.

I staggered forward, dazed. It felt as if my head had been gashed open and I sensed vaguely that I had broken a couple of fingers on my left hand. The chair had split in half with the force of the blow. Mervyn retreated before my staggering advance as though I was capable of assaulting him. Sam stepped forward.

'You bloody fool!' he hissed at his companion. Then he took the remnants of the chair out of his unresisting hands, contemptuously ripped off a dangling leg, stepped forward another pace and swung it viciously at the side of my neck.

I fell into blackness.

THIRTEEN

Some time later, I didn't know how long, I awoke into a blackness which at first seemed as dense as my unconsciousness but gradually eased into grey.

I was weak and faint and spent what seemed ages struggling to get into a sitting position before I realized that it wasn't just weakness which hindered me.

My hands were tied behind my back and hobbled to my ankles.

I was lying on a stone floor and as my eyes became used to the greyness I realized I was in some kind of boiler-room. I could see the outlines of the great metal boiler against the wall opposite. Behind me was a pile of coke and it was by rolling against this that I finally got to a kneeling position which was the nearest to being upright I could manage.

The pain from the jagged pieces of coke pressing into my knees was sharp enough to penetrate the violent throbbing which filled my head, but I held the position long enough to look around and locate the door up a couple of steps and to my left. Beneath it was a thin sliver of light which, much diluted, provided my illumination.

With a sense of having accomplished something, I subsided on to the pile of coke, which slid down around me in a rustling avalanche. The noise must have penetrated the door for a couple of seconds later it was flung open.

'He's awake,' I heard Mervyn's voice say.

'Well, hit him again.' Cooper.

'No. I can't. Not when he's tied up.'

I heard a chair moved impatiently, then determined footsteps across a wooden floor and down the steps. Next moment my hair was seized in a vicious grasp and my head forced back till I was looking Sam full in the face.

He laid a piece of wood, probably the chair leg, against my bruised and swollen neck. I tried to speak but only then realized the full effect of his first blow. I could only produce a choked gurgle. He smiled as he became aware of my predicament and let me drop back on to the coke.

'What are we going to do with him, Sam?' came Mervyn's fearful voice from the doorway.

I lay coiled up like a foetus on the coke and strained my ears for the answer.

'Kill him.'

I wished I hadn't bothered.

'Kill him,' echoed Mervyn. 'But you said before we might just take him to the police and say we captured him. They'd never believe his story, not with more of us. That's what you said.'

His voice was getting higher. Sam cut in.

'I thought a bit more. He's dangerous. He'll talk and talk till someone gets interested. If he disappears that's practically proof he's guilty.'

His tone of voice was conversational, casual. I began to suspect he must be that happily rare monster, the pure sadist. But he stooped over me once more, and his mouth and eyes belied his coldly logical words. He looked about thirteen, desperately struggling with a problem beyond his years and longing to be advised, but too stubborn to ask.

I tried to speak again, but produced only another grunt and Mervyn's voice cut across it.

'What about his wife?'

Sam adjusted his face, though he couldn't hide the uncertainty in his eyes, and turned away from me.

'That bird? Who'll listen to her? She's biased. I think he might have been bluffing about her anyway.'

His voice was as cool as ever, with just a hint of amusement in it. But it rang artificially to me now; I could trace its source to a dozen television series.

175

For a moment, the thought gave me comfort; comfort which increased as Mervyn spoke once more.

'But we can't just kill him, Sam.'

His voice was almost hysterical now with protest.

'Are you chickening out again, Merv?' asked Cooper softly.

The tones were still the tones of the television master criminal. But now their artificiality brought me little relief. It had begun to dawn on me that playing a role doesn't make any of the actions involved in that role less real.

And Mervyn's reluctance, my major source of hope only a minute earlier, was now obviously the main reagent to harden Cooper in his role. The needs and wishes of others can make us deny our real selves in all kinds of strange ways. I thought briefly of myself and Peter, but self-analysis was an unwarranted luxury at that particular moment.

'I never did, Sam. You know I never,' protested Mervyn.

Sam moved away, then in a resigned tone as if in answer to some pleading expression on Mervyn's face he said, 'Oh, bring him up if you like then. I don't care.'

Footsteps came down and Mervyn half lifted me. He caught hold of my cracked hand and I let out a strangled shriek.

'Sorry,' he said. Then I was manhandled up the steps into a small kitchen which I took to be an appendage of the hall. When Mervyn let me go, I just collapsed sideways again of course. He rummaged in a drawer and produced a large knife. For a second I thought that in an effort to conciliate Sam, who sat on a stool by the sink looking down at me with disdain, he was going to cut my throat. But he only sawed at the rope which linked my wrists and my ankles. Having cut through this, he helped me to a sitting position with my back against the wall. My ankles and wrists were still tightly bound, but the relief of being able to stretch out my legs made even the agony of cramp seem pleasurable. Mervyn filled a cup with water and set it to my lips. I took a mouthful and swallowed painfully. Then another.

176

'You know what they say about lambs, Merv,' said Sam suddenly. 'You should never make a pet of one or it will really upset you when you take it to the market.'

Mervyn ignored him and continued to hold the cup to my lips till I shook my head.

'Time,' I said to him. 'What time?'

He looked at his watch.

'Five to eleven.'

I must have been unconscious almost an hour.

'I'll have to be getting home soon, Sam,' said Mervyn, his voice betraying a longing to get back to the familiar surroundings and see the familiar faces at his home.

'Me too,' said Sam. 'Let's get it over with. You or me?'

'What?'

'Kill him. It's about time you had a go. I do all the rough work round here.'

'I can't, Sam. Honest, I can't.'

Cooper shrugged.

'All right.'

He stood up and opened a cupboard, reached in and produced a white tablecloth. He came purposefully towards me and draped it over the floor around me.

'What's that for?' enquired Mervyn.

'Blood,' said Sam laconically, then held his hand out like a surgeon in the theatre.

'Let's have the knife,' he said.

It was all so dreadfully corny that I could not quite take it seriously. I could see from Sam's face that he did not know either just how serious he was. I think he was hoping almost as desperately as I was for something to interrupt the situation.

Only Mervyn was completely convinced of the seriousness of what was happening. And ironically, the more convinced *he* was, the more likely it was to happen.

'No, Sam,' he said. 'No.'

'Give us it here then,' said Sam impatiently, and reached back and snatched the knife up from the floor.

'Now, Mr Bentink,' he said.

I am still not sure if he would have used it or not. I don't think so. His face was full of trouble.

But Mervyn had no doubts.

'No, Sam!' he cried, and swung the discarded chair leg against Cooper's skull just above the ear with a terrible smack. His face went grey in front of me, the knife fell, and he collapsed over my legs.

I kicked him away. He twisted round on to his back and lay with unseeing eyes staring at the ceiling. A slowly swelling bubble of saliva oozed from his lips.

Mervyn bent over him.

'Sam. Oh, Sam,' he said.

I didn't like this at all. I had a feeling that any uncertainties which might have existed in Sam's mind would have disappeared when he regained consciousness. Temporarily, anyway, he would have no doubts about his role. And temporarily could mean forever for me.

'Mervyn,' I croaked, 'untie me, Mervyn. I can help you. There was no point unless you untie me, Mervyn.'

I was probably half unintelligible anyway, but he did not even acknowledge that I was making sounds. He just knelt there cradling Sam's head and weeping.

I looked around desperately. Then I remembered the knife. It lay where it had fallen and I let myself slide slowly down the wall till my hands could reach it. The blade was too long for me to be able to hold it in my hand and saw at the rope binding my wrists so I concentrated on that between my ankles. It took a surprisingly long time. I thought with horror of Sam sawing away at my throat with this blunt blade and a memory came to me of Peter killing the sheep. It seemed an infinity away.

I staggered to my feet, hands still tied behind my back, and stumbled across to the door. I was bent on putting as much distance between myself and this blond-haired, blue-eyed youth who lay unconscious on the floor. I had never been so frightened of anyone in my life. I turned my back to the door and twisted the handle.

It was locked.

I looked around for a key but could see nothing. It seemed to me as if there was more colour in Sam's cheeks. The saliva bubble had burst.

Desperately, and foolishly in my weakened condition, I began thrusting at the door with my shoulder.

'Mr Bentink.'

I spun round in terror. It was Mervyn.

'Mr Bentink.'

'Open the door, Mervyn.'

I could hardly understand my own voice.

'Mr Bentink. You've got to help me. I don't know what happened. It wasn't right. It wasn't what I thought.'

'Open the door, Mervyn, please.'

Had Sam stirred? No, it was just nerves.

'I'd never done it before, not properly. Sam had. Sam told me what it was like. And I'd read about it. And seen pictures. Sam had some. We talked about girls a lot on holiday. Especially those two – Sam said they were ready for it. He said he knew.'

Sam moved. There was no mistaking it this time.

'Mervyn, cut my arms loose. Hurry.'

He ignored my plea but stood in front of me looking vacantly at the floor.

'We met them on the mountain. They were half undressed. I couldn't stop looking at them all the time we were talking. I just couldn't help it. One of them said something to Sam and he made a joke. We all laughed. I wanted to touch them, that's all. Just touch.'

Sam suddenly turned over and lay on his side. I could not tell how much this was a conscious move, how much some kind of reflex. I did not want to find out. I decided to try the window, but Mervyn gripped me by my jacket with surprising strength. Or perhaps it was just my surprising weakness.

'Sam put his arm round one, I mean right round so that his hand touched her breast. She stopped laughing. She wanted to go but he wouldn't let her. He just laughed. He held her and with his other hand he undid her bra, then pulled it off. She tried to cover herself with her hands but we all saw. We all saw. It was the first time I had. Really I mean. Not pictures.'

Sam raised himself on his elbow. His eyes looked fully alert.

'Sam got hold of her again and held her arms behind her back so we could all see. The other one tried to help, but I grabbed her and one of the others pulled her bra off. They started to shout but we put our hands over their mouths. Then Sam took her shorts off and got on top of her and started to do it. He was holding her round the throat so she couldn't scream. He started to do it and he shouted at me to start. I couldn't help it. I thought she probably wanted it anyway like Sam said. So I did it. The others helped hold her and she sort of fainted. Then Sam finished and he got up and I finished too and I got up. And Sam said it was someone else's turn. But when one of the others went over to his girl he said she wasn't breathing. He said she was dead. He said Sam had squeezed her throat too hard.'

I looked with fascinated horror at Sam, who had risen unsteadily to his feet and was casting around for a weapon. The knife lay where I had dropped it.

'He came over to mine then. She was still breathing all right. He asked if anyone else wanted to do it with her. But no one did, not any more. Then he laughed and he said that he couldn't let one of them go when we'd killed the other. And he squeezed her throat. Till she stopped breathing.'

Sam had the knife in his hand. Mervyn relaxed his grip. All animation had left his voice.

'Then we got all their stuff together and we dragged them across to a gully. We tipped them in. I didn't know what to do. No one did except Sam. He remembered seeing you earlier. We all did. We hadn't met anyone else and

180

you were dressed funny. Not funny. But not like us. We could remember, see? So we all made up our story. We didn't know you had seen them. We just wanted to fool the police. We just said we saw them with two men. Then they started asking a lot more closely. They kept on hinting at you. So Sam changed the story a bit to fit you more. Sam changed it for us all.'

So I hadn't been altogether wrong, but I had no time now for idle speculation. Sam, who had for the past couple of moments been listening attentively to Mervyn, suddenly moved. I poised myself to dodge without much hope. The knife swung back, then thrust forward. I remained perfectly still.

'Sam,' said Mervyn, his hand clawing up his back to where the hilt protruded. 'Sam.'

Then he fell forward and Sam and I faced each other. I looked at his face, twisted out of all recognition by a snarl of anger; or pain; or madness. To me it didn't much matter which. I fell back against the door wrestling with the cords which bound my wrists.

He began to laugh.

It was contrast, not similarity, which brought to my mind that melodic line of laughter drifting up the fellside an eternity ago. The sun had been shining, we had seemed isolated from time, only joy lay behind and ahead. And the laughter of a couple of youngsters in that peaceful scene had not seemed a discordant noise.

The noise I heard now was a ragged, thin-edged bark which spiralled rapidly to an almost noiseless expulsion of air through the twisted funnel of his mouth. I called upon Superboy deep inside me to lash out with a well-aimed kick. But Superboy was not coming out to play.

I began to slide down the door. I had no desire to end up on the floor, but I had no muscular control in the face of this terrible effigy of youth who was surely about to strangle me. In another moment I knew my bowels would open, but there was nothing I could do about it.

I closed my eyes and prayed that the door would burst open and the police rush in. They could arrest me, charge me, try me, condemn me. I would fall in front of Copley and kiss his feet as they spurned me.

But there was no cracking of wood as the door splintered open. Only a new sound, like but unlike the insane laughter I had just heard.

I opened my eyes again.

Sam was still standing before me, his face contorted. But now he was crying. At first he sobbed as hysterically as he had laughed, but gradually the sobs died away, though the tears still poured down his cheeks and seemed to smooth his features back to their proper youthfulness.

He knelt beside Mervyn.

'Merv,' he said. 'Merv. Answer me.'

He tried to turn his friend over on his back, but the knife prevented this. With a curiously gentle force he drew it out. No fresh blood flowed from the wound. I knew he was dead.

Consciousness of this must have come to Sam too for he made no further attempts to turn the dead boy over, but merely laid him gently back on to the floor.

He then squatted on his haunches, absently hefting the knife in his hand.

I had regained a little of my strength and struggled to a sitting position.

He's looking for someone to blame, I thought in new horror, and began to try to struggle upright.

'Mr Bentink,' said Sam.

I was up on one knee. An uneven edge of floorboard was cutting into the knee on which all my weight pressed. But I ignored the pain and knelt in perfect stillness.

'Mr Bentink,' said Sam again. He too was still on his knees by Mervyn. He looked at me, his mouth opened and shut a couple of times, but no words came out. Then, as if deciding the effort was not worth it, he shrugged his shoulders, gave me a smile of great charm, and with the same gentleness he

182

had used when handling his friend's body, he turned my own unresisting frame around.

At that moment I knew what it meant to be absolute for death. Time had stopped a second away from my heartbeat. There was no blinding vision of eternal truth, no rapid unwinding of all the reels of my life before me. Just a horror that it should come to this, that thirty-three years of life should lead to this. Every sense was deadened. Not even Shakespeare could have written any last words I would have cared to speak at that moment.

Then I realized as suddenly and completely that I wasn't dying, that something quite different was happening.

Sam was sawing away at my bonds.

For a second I thought some miraculous change had taken place in the boy.

Then I started to listen to what he was saying.

'You shouldn't have killed Mervyn, Mr Bentink, and tried to murder me too. Isn't it lucky that I'm going to be able to escape and fetch help. It'll only take a couple of minutes. I'd try to get away if I were you. I'll bring Merv's dad. He's very big and very excitable.'

I twisted away violently. Suddenly I didn't want my bonds cut. He just kept on smiling and came towards me again.

Then my earlier prayer was belatedly answered. There came a hammering from the door behind me, followed by a splintering as somebody shoulder-charged it. It all happened so quickly that I did not have time to get out of the way and as it burst open the door caught me on the back and spun me against the wall in a sitting position. Sam with the speed of a cat had leapt across the room, flinging away the knife as he did so, and was sitting in the far corner cowering like a maltreated animal.

'Help me,' he cried piteously. 'He's killed Merv. Don't let him touch me.'

He held out his arms beseechingly. I looked round.

Standing in the doorway, backed by a whole posse of

uniformed policemen, was Copley. I did not feel so inclined now to embrace his feet.

He looked at the bloody scene before him with a dangerous glitter in his eyes. I was once again trying to struggle to my feet. Copley strode towards me. If I had been expecting assistance his face should have disabused me. His left hand thrust me back against the wall.

'You bastard!' he said, almost conversationally, as his right fist smashed twice into my stomach. I retched violently and fell forward as his left hand let go. The room was full of people now, I was dimly aware. I faintly heard a voice say, 'Inspector! this man's hands are tied.'

'Let me see,' came Copley's rasping tones, and I was seized again and the cords round my wrists were pulled at savagely.

There was an area of my mind still cool enough to realize that what Copley had believed – and now still hoped – was that I had killed Mervyn and somehow tied my own arms behind my back in an effort to demonstrate my innocence. He might even have got the cords off, had not he been interrupted.

'I think perhaps there are too many people in this room, Inspector,' said a voice I remembered.

It was Melton.

Copley stood up immediately and began to give orders rapidly, efficiently. I twisted my head round as the pain in my belly began to ease. Melton knelt beside me. His hands quickly, expertly, tested the bindings on my wrists, then he produced a pen-knife from his pocket and sawed through the cord.

The pain I experienced as I tried to massage some life back into my hands was worse even than Copley's assault. Melton led me out of the kitchen into the main hall. We had to step carefully round Mervyn's body. I did not care to look.

We sat down on hard chairs of the same type which Mervyn had smashed over my back. Melton offered me one of my own cigarettes, taking them from my pocket when he saw my ineffectual attempts to extract the packet. Then he leaned forward and adjusted his spectacles to the uttermost tip of his nose.

'Now, Mr Bentink,' he said. I recognized in that 'now' the beginnings of a lengthy, searching interrogation. I shook my head. It probably looked as if I was trying to clear my mind, but in fact it was a simple negative. I had had enough. I had been attacked, beaten, punched, bound, and terrified beyond despair. Let someone else give the answers.

I said clearly and slowly, 'Sam killed the girls. Ask the others.'

Then I fainted. I had decided to faint in any case and refuse to open my eyes till I was in a hospital bed, drugged and bathed and hygienically wrapped. But once I made the decision, it proved to make no great call on my acting ability, and I slid away effortlessly into a welcome darkness.

FOURTEEN

I half woke from time to time I remember as I was moved to the hospital in Carlisle, but I resolutely fought my way back into oblivion until I found my head resting on a pillow and my body warm under bedclothes.

At the bottom of the bed stood a police-constable. He looked down at me impassively. I felt I recognized him and half-smiled. He nodded carefully and went out of the door.

I looked around and saw that I had a room to myself. This, I assumed, was one of the perks of being of interest to the police. The window curtains were still closed, but strong sunlight was obviously leaning up against them. I must have slept all night, I decided.

The door opened and Jan came in. She looked very tired. She sat on the edge of the bed and for a few moments we said nothing.

'Is it over?' I finally asked.

She shrugged.

'I don't think it will ever be over,' she replied. I did not feel in the mood for philosophical analysis, so asked,

'What happened last night?'

'The police stopped me after a few miles. So much for my notion of getting right down to London.'

'And then?'

'They talked to me. That man Copley came. Then Melton. Finally I told them all I knew. And they headed back to Wyrton.'

I thought this over carefully.

'They didn't seem very convinced of my innocence when they arrived.'

She shrugged again. I could see she was very tired indeed.

'Innocent, guilty, it seemed best in the end just to tell them where you were. They were beginning to have pretty firm suspicions anyway.'

There was a tap at the door and Melton came in.

'Good morning, Mr Bentink. Better now, I hope, Mrs Bentink? You really ought to get some sleep now, you know.'

'I'll wait,' said Janet.

'Very well.'

'What's happened, Superintendent?' I asked with a smile. I had decided not to rub it in too much that he had been mistaken from the start. I felt a vague general benevolence and stretched my limbs luxuriously under the sheets. Melton did not smile back.

'We have questioned the other boys again. When they heard what had happened to the boy Mervyn they co-operated fully and we have the whole story. It does not make pleasant hearing.'

'What will happen to the boys?' Jan asked.

'That is not up to me, Mrs Bentink. Some form of probationary care, an attempt to assess what damage this business has done to them. Their culpability is linked closely with their fear. They are very young and were very afraid. Of the deed. Of Sam.'

'Of the police,' I could not resist saying.

'Of the police, certainly. But there are those much older with much less real cause for fear who have acted with as much, if not more, childish irrationality.'

I sat up at this.

'If that is meant for me, Superintendent . . .'

'You must take it as you will, Mr Bentink. In any case you will be gratified to hear that it is unlikely that any charges will be brought against you.'

I flung back the bedclothes and sat up on the edge of the bed. I was seething with an indignation which I tried hard to control before it became ludicrous to behold.

'No charge against me? Well, thank you, Superintendent. I'm sorry I am not able to offer the police the same reassurance.'

'I'm not sure what you mean, sir.'

My benevolence had evaporated; my late resolve to be a good winner had disappeared entirely.

'Listen, Superintendent. I have been wrongly arrested, I have been pursued at peril to my life and limb over some of the most dangerous countryside in the land, I have suffered privation and hardship, my friends and relatives have suffered considerable pain of mind at my predicament, and last but not least, I have been brutally assaulted by that man Copley who is totally unfit to be a police-officer.'

Melton was quite unmoved by my outburst. He merely moved his spectacles an eighth of an inch up the bridge of his nose and walked across the room to draw the curtains. The morning sun flowed in and made me blink as it glistened off the starched whiteness of the bed-linen. A few minutes ago I might have taken this infusion of light and warmth as a symbol of the settlement of the affair. But now I was in no mood for symbols.

'Well, Melton?'

He turned round and sighed.

'Mr Bentink, you say you were wrongfully arrested. You have never been arrested to the best of my knowledge.'

I laughed.

'A verbal quibble. Why, you even started to charge me.'

'You must be mistaken. There is no record of a charge having been made.'

'Only because you never finished it. I had the sense to get out.'

He sighed patiently.

'If I remember rightly, Mr Bentink, I interviewed you alone in Keswick. All the time. I could hardly charge you without a witness now, could I?'

I remembered what Ferguson had said. But I still hadn't finished.

188

'You cannot deny the hunt for me. That was rather too public, wasn't it?'

'Of course we looked for you, Mr Bentink. Can you blame us? You are connected, however tenuously, with a most brutal crime. You escape dramatically and go rushing off into the mountains. Of course we pursue you. We would not be doing our duty if we did not pursue you. You say we put your life and limbs in peril. You do not consider that by acting in this way, you put in danger the life of every man who joined in the search. They also had to scramble around the fells, you know.'

I opened my mouth to speak, but he waved aside my attempt at interruption. He was more animated than I had seen him in our brief acquaintance.

'As for bad publicity, that was of your own making too. If you feel you have a case for libel, take it up with the newspapers concerned. All the police do is hand out facts, descriptions. Nor can you blame us for causing mental pain to those close to you. You seem to be able to manage that very well without our aid, in any case.'

There was a pause. Janet was looking steadfastly at the floor. Melton spoke again.

'I'm sorry. I had no right to say that.'

I didn't want to enter into any kind of discussion on these lines. I tried to stir some fresh life into my flagging indignation.

'You can't deny Copley's assault. And his aggressive attitude, Superintendent.'

Now he exploded.

'No, but I will justify it. More easily than I believe you can justify your assault of one of my constables in Keswick.'

I shifted uneasily.

'How is he?'

'I thought you would never ask, Mr Bentink,' he replied with heavy irony. 'It's not like a film on the television, you know, Mr Bentink. When you hit a man, or kick a man, the damage can be great. And permanent.'

I felt sick.

'Fortunately this was not the case here. Indeed you had the ocular proof of the constable's well-being when you awoke this morning.'

I remembered how familiar his face had been. No wonder he had not returned my smile.

'Superintendent,' I began.

'Yes.'

'Nothing.'

Jan looked up.

'I think that you have made my husband look at things in a new light, Superintendent. You seem to be sharing out responsibility between you. We know who killed the girls. But just who was responsible for the death of that boy last night?'

This was the question I had wanted to ask. Melton had obviously thought about this too.

'You will appreciate I am not speaking now as a police-officer, Mrs Bentink. Obviously part of the responsibility lies with your husband. He it was who directly initiated the events of last night. But their outcome was unforeseeable. By the same token, you yourself are in part responsible.'

Janet started slightly, then nodded.

'You could have acted with more common sense than you did; you could have co-operated more quickly when we stopped you; you could have put personal loyalty a little lower down the list – or a little higher perhaps.

'But ultimately it is my responsibility and one I must bear alone. It makes things worse to admit I was not without suspicions. It makes things worse that one of my subordinates was so convinced of your guilt that he too readily accepted the boys' corroborating story.'

'And Sam himself. Whose responsibility is that?'

'For what he is? I don't know.'

'And for what happens to him now?'

'Not mine, I'm glad to say,' Melton said with heart-felt relief.

190

'Glad? For your sake? Or his?'

'My own. And his too, I think. I saw those girls, talked to their parents. For all our sakes it's better that someone else takes over now.'

There was silence for a while, broken only when I stood up and walked to the window. It overlooked an unimaginatively laid-out garden in the hospital courtyard, but the brilliant sunshine touched everything with its magic. Even us, I supposed, feeling the warmth seeping through my pyjamas.

'I'll go now.'

I turned and saw Melton at the door. I had the impression he had just said something to Jan.

'There's still a great deal we must talk about, Mr Bentink. But later will do. By the way, there were two other crimes of yours I didn't mention.'

There was a humorous twist to his lips. He was obviously going to exit on a joke.

'What?'

'Damaging a police-station. And the assault on Mrs Reckitt. You made quite a hole in that window. But I think our funds can run to a little glass.'

'And Mrs Reckitt?'

He grinned broadly. He looked quite different.

'I began to have my doubts when I visited her myself to ask some questions. After ten minutes or so, she offered to re-enact the crime with me.'

He went out chuckling.

I didn't laugh. Nothing in my memory of Moira Jane made me want to laugh. Nor did Janet, who now stood up in her turn.

'I think I'll go and get some sleep now, Harry.'

'All right,' I said.

'We've got a lot to talk about and I'd like to be awake when we talk,' she said.

I made no move to stop her and she left.

The next few days were very full. I was allowed out of

bed and spent a great deal of time talking to Melton. I don't think either of us became fonder of the other. He was just interested in sorting out facts for his records. I pursued my vendetta with Copley, trying to get Melton to admit that his inspector had put the idea of claiming they had seen us into the boys' minds. But he remained adamant that the boys themselves had first mentioned seeing the girls with someone else at a distance.

'It's the kind of over-elaboration of detail the naïve criminal often invents to turn attention away from himself. It was an unhappy coincidence that you two did in fact meet the girls; and lied about it.'

'But you can't deny the boys' minds were directed to us?'

'Yes, I'm sorry to say. That I must admit. Someone said too much too early. But if you had told the truth in the first place, you realize that their alleged sighting over an hour later would have in fact provided you with some kind of alibi?'

I couldn't argue with this. Melton did, however, gratify me by telling me he did not think I would be required to give any evidence other than my statement. I had no desire to see Sam again.

I spent even more time talking to Janet; perhaps too much. We were both desperately eager to capitalize on the renewed intimacy of the past few days. But, as we had feared, the momentum was failing and there were things between us which talking could not destroy. Whereas earlier she had appeared to take Moira Reckitt and Annie Ferguson in her stride, now she kept on coming back to them and probing to her own pain and my irritation. I had a note from Moira inviting me to visit her. I did not go. As for Annie, her father had taken her off to a conference of birdmen in America with a haste that indicated to me he wanted to keep her out of my way for as long as possible. At least that made matters a little simpler.

But the biggest obstacle was still Peter. He was no longer

in the prison hospital, of course, but had returned to the nursing home for more treatment. I was anxious to visit him but when I mentioned this to Jan, she shook her head firmly.

'No,' she said. 'No. I'd rather you didn't.'

She was trembling. I was taken aback by her opposition.

'Look,' I explained, 'I just want to see him. He's sick. I feel I'm partly responsible. But he'll never come between us again, I promise you. I just want to make this one visit, to explain if possible. If not, to say "goodbye".'

But she would not budge.

'If you go, it starts again,' she said. 'I know. It's too soon. You must give him a chance to be himself by himself. It's too soon, Harry, I know.'

'You talk as if you'd seen him,' I said.

'I have. Last week. You mustn't go, Harry. We need to recover as much as Peter. Give us a chance together. If you don't, I may have to look for it alone. Don't go yet.'

Superboy could not resist such a challenge. I went the next day.

I was taken by a male nurse to a small room at the blank end of a long corridor.

'He knows you're coming,' said the nurse. 'He's been very excited all day.'

I opened the door and went in. Peter was combing his hair in front of a metal mirror. His eyes filled with delight as he turned and saw me.

'Harry,' he said, 'Harry. This is great. Come and sit down. Let's talk.'

We talked for half an hour, carefully never touching upon the murders. It was easier than I expected and I was impressed by his appearance of normality. He was a little thinner, a little paler, but in every other respect quite himself. Several times I was on the brink of referring to the Lake District, but the doctor I had seen had been very positive that I must not do this, so I kept silence. But I resolved to have another word with the doctor before I left.

Also the task of explaining to Peter that I put Janet before him, that in order to save my marriage I must see considerably less of him, began to seem fairly easy. I had not discussed this with the doctor, but in the end I took my courage in my hands and told him.

His reaction was perfectly normal. He looked a little downcast, but then smiled at me and said, 'Of course, I understand, Harry. You're quite right. But I will still see you sometimes, won't I?'

I reassured him, then with a sense of a job well done, I stood up to go.

'Goodbye, Peter,' I said.

'Goodbye, Harry.'

I turned. His hand caught at my arm.

'Harry,' he said in a low voice, 'don't forget me. We've been through a lot together. Do you remember how we killed the sheep? And then the girls? Do you remember that, Harry? The sheep. Those girls. Remember!'

His voice had risen and his grip on my arm tightened till it was painful. I broke away, the door opened and the nurse came in.

'Don't leave me yet, Harry,' said Peter. 'Don't leave me. You will come back, won't you? Please come back.'

I went out into the corridor and his voice followed me, made even more moving by the curious flat quality given it by the yielding walls.

The doctor listened attentively to my account. To my surprise he did not seem very perturbed when I told him of Peter's final words.

'He doesn't really believe that he killed those girls, you see,' he explained. 'He confessed in the first place as a way out, a means of relieving pressure. It's surprising what even the most well-balanced of us will do or say at moments of stress.'

'Surprising?' I asked. 'No, not so surprising to me, doctor.'

He raised his eyebrows sardonically at me and went on,

'Also, in Mr Thorne's case, there is this desire to be linked with you. I suspect the police told him you had confessed, and that his own confession, as well as relieving pressure, also gave him a chance to join you.'

'What will happen now?'

He smiled confidently.

'I have no worries. Peter will be fit and well again in a couple of months with your help.'

'And without it?'

He looked disconcerted. Briefly I explained.

'Your wife is right to a certain extent. Certainly your visits to Peter will increase his dependency on you. It could hardly be otherwise. Don't misunderstand me. He's not so sick that he won't recover without you. It'll take longer. All that will happen will be that he'll find a suitable substitute. Reliable. Solid. Dependable.' He laughed. 'Probably me.'

'At least you're qualified, doctor.'

'Yes. I'm qualified.'

The very tonelessness with which he said this struck me as a comment on my attitude, but I left without further discussion.

I had to get back to Carlisle where Jan was still staying and talk things over from the start again.

But when I got back, Janet was gone. She left a note for me.

'Harry, I'm leaving. Don't think it's because of Peter. I'm desperately sorry for him and hope he will be well again soon. But I honestly think he'll be better without you. I'm rather like him, perhaps that's why we never got on. I needed you, need you, I don't know. But there's something in you which isn't good for us, for me, for him. A kind of self-regarding. I think that's probably why you survived out on the fells. I thought for a while there was a change and hope for us. But all that really happened was that I got caught up in your orbit just like all the others. You belong to the moment only, Harry. I need wider horizons.'

It ended there, abruptly, enigmatically.

But not enigmatically enough for my self-esteem.

I spent a feverish week trying to track her down. No one could help. Will and Mary were sympathetic but unsurprised. Melton dismissed me with polite speed when I sought his assistance. Our London friends knew nothing. She had been back to the flat, I knew. One or two personal belongings had gone – a statuette; a picture. I wept dry tears when I saw the gaps they left. But the realization that she meant to go for good did not strike home until the third day after my return to London. Shattock, the man who looks after the garage under our block of flats, approached me as I left one morning. He touched his scant forelock in a gesture more offensive than humble and said, 'Excuse me, Mr Bentink. I wonder if Mrs Bentink would mind moving her car.'

I thought for one heart-turning moment that Jan must have come back. Then he went on.

'It's just a bit out of line, you see. Not worth bothering about really, but it's been like that a week now and if it's going to be left standing, it might as well be up to the wall so as not to inconvenience the other tenants.'

I hardly heard what he was saying as I strode rapidly down into the garage with Shattock puffing behind me. It was a large underground garage but I had no difficulty in spotting Jan's Mini. It looked as if it had been parked in a hurry and just left. I should certainly have noticed it if I had been down there since my return, but I rarely drove in London. The keys were still in the ignition, the door was unlocked. I looked at Shattock's insultingly helpful face. He must have noticed the keys.

'Why didn't you move it yourself?'

'Oh, I couldn't have done that, sir, not without the lady's permission and she don't seem to have been around lately.'

He knew. They must all know, everyone who worked in the building. It was something to enjoy. But I had no desire to reflect upon the petty malice of the human animal at that moment. All I knew, all I could think was that if Jan had left her car, she had gone for good. She was not so stupid as to leave clothes, shoes, anything of that ilk; she needed those: they were hers by right. But the car, her Mini, was her most treasured possession and the most cherished of my gifts. To abandon it was to abandon me.

I climbed in and moved the car right up to the wall, got out, locked the door and walked away, ignoring Shattock's fulsome thank-yous.

My mind was in a turmoil. In my mail that morning there had been a note from Peter's doctor asking if I could call to see him, and a short letter, conventionally, almost stiltedly, phrased, from Annie expressing her pleasure at the news which had just reached her.

In addition to this, though I was less pestered by reporters than I had been, a couple of the papers (those, strangely enough, which had previously been most blatant in their assumption of my guilt), still pursued me with 'generous' offers for the exclusive rights on the story of my 'ordeal'. Even if I had felt tempted to accept, my solicitor had advised me to regard every aspect of the affair as *sub judice*. Not that his warning was needed. I had no desire at all to do business with these or any newspapers. I didn't need the money, I didn't want the publicity. But still they persisted.

So when I got to my office that morning, my nerves were stretched taut. The new perspective I thought I had found in the mountains had rapidly wavered and gone out of focus.

Not wholly, but mainly as a result of my prolonged 'holiday', a great deal of extremely urgent business had piled up for me, and far from being able to relegate to his proper subservient position that 'me' which was a pin-striped business man, 'he' had begun to make new and greater demands on my life.

Or perhaps it was just that my life had other more important demands being made on it at the same time. I could do no work that morning and after a couple of hours I dropped everything and went home, determined to look at my problems.

Not that there was much to look at. It is always a pleasant illusion to tell ourselves that it is other people who concern us. But it is an illusion difficult to preserve.

I told myself I was bothered about what happened to Jan. To Peter. To Annie, to a lesser extent, I suppose.

To myself to a greater extent, I should have added.

For in the end, after twenty-four hours' 'looking' at the problem, I did what I had done in Keswick police-station without any looking at all.

I ran.

I stayed long enough to delegate all essential authority in the firm.

I told my friends that I had been medically directed to take a change of air, my colleagues that I hoped to establish new business contacts abroad, wrote an apologetic letter to Peter's doctor.

And left.

I was sick of it all, of worrying, of working, of effort, of decisions. I wanted a world of acquaintances, of transient relationships, for a while. As my boat crossed the Channel and I peered down at the white scar of our wake on the sea's grey skin, I even managed to tell myself that I had done my bit for long enough. It was time for others to act.

That was more than six months ago. I think then I half believed that what had happened would heal up as quickly and leave as little trace as that gash of bursting foam. But even then I half disbelieved also. I wandered slowly across the face of Europe. I could afford to. I even turned my imagined business dealings into reality and this helped to satisfy my need for self-justification. But like a chronic disease, it broke out again. And again. Eventually I found myself explaining to acquaintances as casual as I could have desired, and being hurt by their lack of interest.

I had had enough by Christmas, most of which I spent in a Hamburg bar and the rest of which I spent somewhere which involved the spending of every penny I had, though whether it was church or brothel I never knew. I was incapable of behaving properly in either. I would have gone home then but I had by now mapped out a kind of touring business programme for myself and some stubbornness of will made me go on. I was like a marathon-runner who doesn't stop because there's nowhere to stay. But like a runner I found that the first step past endurance is the hardest. The physical image was a very real one for I found that more and more I was beginning to feel as I had done out on the fells those two nights last summer.

Finally with spring I turned and headed back. Not home, not London, but here, once more to the Lakes. The newspapers had pestered me relentlessly but in vain for the right to tell my story. And now I wanted to tell it my way, to make my experiences reliveable, for it is the frightening transience of experience which makes us what we are. Or makes us remain what we are. So I came back to these hills, these waters, these memories.

This morning I wrote a letter to Peter's doctor offering my help for what it is worth. I know he is out and working again, but I am not sure how he will react to me. I doubt if I have been much of a friend to him. I don't know if I ever can be now, but I see no escape from trying, for his sake this time, not for mine. I wrote the letter also because I have to make it quite clear here what I have done, what I shall do.

Yesterday I drove into Penrith and went to see Chief-Superintendent Melton. This again was something I felt needed doing. He greeted me, with no surprise, but sat me down and enquired politely after my health and my affairs. I told him a great deal more than I intended but, I felt, even less than he knew. He in his turn told me what I had already read, that Sam had been sentenced to life, whatever that might mean. He was, it seemed, sane within the terms of the law. The other four surviving members of the Wyrton Boys' Club party had been kept under careful psychiatric observation since the previous summer. Two of the families concerned had moved from the village and the boys had adjusted happily and normally to their new environment.

Of the other two, one boy had had to be removed from his parents whose narrow religious views were quite incapable of comprehending events of this nature. They themselves were moved almost to despair by their conviction of their son's damnation and this not unnaturally had affected the boy's health. He was now in a local authority home where he seemed to be settling well. Strangely enough, his removal – and that of the first two – seemed to have affected most of all the one lad remaining in the village. His parents, good reasonable people, were growing more and more concerned by his withdrawal into himself and it was thought that he too might have to be removed for treatment.

There seemed little left to say after this and the meeting was breaking up on this sombre note when Melton seemed to come to a decision. Adjusting his spectacles in that characteristic way, he coughed and said, 'By the way, I hear Mrs Bentink is with us again, staying with her parents for a while. I hope the weather holds out for you both. The rain seems to have retreated, temporarily at least.'

Then he ushered me out into the corridor and shook me by the hand.

'I'm glad you called. I wondered if you would,' he said.

As I left, I think I saw Copley driving off outside. He didn't look round.

Well, that's it all. My first impulse was to drive right round to Thurbeck and I even set off. But after only a couple of miles I halted and turned back to my hotel in Buttermere.

This was what I had been writing for, after all. To explain myself, partly to myself. But also to you, Jan. So I must not spoil things, or falsify things by appearing suddenly myself. A long time ago, sitting in a wood outside Wyrton we agreed to tell the truth. And agreed that the truth must be written if it is to remain and be effective as truth. You won't like all you have read. I don't like much of it myself. But it is my truth. And I shall wait here till you let me know whether, knowing the truth, you want to have me with it. I shall wait.